"What's My Body Language Saying?"

"It says you're interested in throwing me over your shoulder and doing very wicked things to me upstairs."

His eyes widened involuntarily. "Wow, you're good. What is *your* body language saying? 'Please hurry'?"

She laughed. "More like, 'Please get over yourself.'"

He matched her grin. "Aww, come on. It's not saying, 'Maybe in a little while, after Mikey's in bed'?" In one move, he landed on the same step with her and a whiff of female curled through his blood. He reached out to trace a finger across her perfect pink lips. "Are you sure?"

Her eyelids drifted halfway closed and she exhaled, leaning ever so slightly toward him. Drawn to him, as he was to her. "I'm...sure."

Her heat wrapped around him, gliding along his nerves.

"Huh. It feels an awful lot like your body language is saying something more like, 'Maybe I'm considering it....'"

* * *

The Baby Deal is part of the #1 bestselling miniseries from Harlequin Desire, Billionaires & Babies: Powerful men... wrapped around their babies' little fingers.

Dear Reader,

I'm sure you've noticed our exciting new look! Harlequin Desire novels will now feature a brand-new cover design, one that perfectly captures the dramatic and sensual stories you love.

Nothing else about the Harlequin Desire books has changed. Inside our pages, you'll still find wealthy alpha heroes caught in unforgettable stories of scandal, secrets and seduction.

Don't miss any of this month's sizzling reads....

CANYON by Brenda Jackson
(The Westmorelands)

DEEP IN A TEXAN'S HEART by Sara Orwig
(Texas Cattleman's Club)

THE BABY DEAL by Kat Cantrell
(Billionaires & Babies)

WRONG MAN, RIGHT KISS by Red Garnier

HIS INSTANT HEIR by Katherine Garbera
(Baby Business)

HIS BY DESIGN by Dani Wade

I hope you're as pleased with our new look as we are. Drop by www.Harlequin.com or use the hash tag #harlequindesire on Twitter to let us know what you think.

Stacy Boyd

Senior Editor

Harlequin Desire

KAT CANTRELL

——

THE BABY DEAL

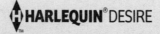

To Stacy Boyd, editor extraordinaire. Thanks for asking me to write this book and then making it so much better, proving once again that we're a great team.

Recycling programs
for this product may
not exist in your area.

ISBN-13: 978-0-373-73260-9

THE BABY DEAL

Copyright © 2013 by Katrina Williams

Printed in U.S.A.

Books by Kat Cantrell

Harlequin Desire

Marriage with Benefits #2212
The Things She Says #2218
The Baby Deal #2247

Other titles by this author available in ebook format.

KAT CANTRELL

read her first Harlequin novel in third grade and has been scribbling in notebooks since she learned to spell. What else would she write but romance? She majored in literature, officially with the intent to teach, but somehow ended up buried in middle management at Corporate America, until she became a stay-at-home mom and full-time writer.

Kat, her husband and their two boys live in North Texas. When she's not writing about characters on the journey to happily-ever-after, she can be found at a soccer game, watching the TV show *Friends* or listening to '80s music.

Kat was the 2011 Harlequin So You Think You Can Write winner and a 2012 RWA Golden Heart finalist for best unpublished series contemporary manuscript.

Dear Reader,

One of my all-time favorite Harlequin Desire titles is a Billionaires and Babies story. When my editor asked me if I'd like to write one, I couldn't say yes fast enough! I love writing about glamorous people and I love babies. All I needed was the perfect billionaire hero. I knew immediately who he'd be.

While researching West Texas for my second book, *The Things She Says,* I stumbled over a huge, fancy airport stuck in the middle of nowhere. I discovered it was actually a space-tourist company where ultra-brave (and ultra-wealthy) civilians pay to go into space—every space enthusiast's dream. I had to explore this in a story.

But what sort of entrepreneur would embark on such a risky business venture, especially considering the expense and the potential danger? He couldn't be ordinary. A superconfident, daredevil billionaire hero burst out of my mind and spilled onto the page. I never caught my breath and I hope Shay leaves you equally as breathless!

I love to hear from readers! Drop me a note through my website: www.katcantrell.com.

Kat

One

Juliana Cane hadn't spoken to Michael Shaylen in eight years, not since the day she'd realized that if she was going to lose him, she'd rather do it on her terms.

And today, when she opened her front door to the man who'd once taken her to heights never experienced before or since, her brain deserted her. She'd practiced a highly appropriate "hello" and a lovely "nice to see you," both suitable greetings for an ex-boyfriend who calls with no warning.

But obviously his brief and to-the-point "I need to talk to you" had knocked her upside down, and she hadn't reoriented yet because all she managed was "You're not on crutches."

Like the last time she'd seen him. A broken leg *did* take less than eight years to heal.

"Day's not over."

A familiar, cloud-parting smile broke open across his stubbly jaw, its effect a forceful punch to a feminine place long forgotten.

Unbelievable. After all this time, both her brain *and* her body still reacted to him without her permission.

"How are you?" he asked. "It's Dr. Cane now, right?"

"Yes." She was a psychologist and thus well equipped to handle this unexpected visit, if the bongo drum in her chest would lay off. "But only my clients call me that. You didn't mention on the phone if you'd be staying long. Do you have time to come in?"

"Sure." He shot a glance toward the long, sleek car idling at the curb.

"Is someone in the car? Everyone is welcome." Even a size-zero supermodel with photo-worthy hair and fourteen thousand dollars' worth of dental work. His usual type, if the media could be believed. "I don't want you to feel awkward about this visit, Michael."

His name stuck in her throat. She'd never called him Michael.

His lips curved into a half grin. "Then stop first-naming me. I'm still Shay."

Shay. His mega-watt personality engulfed the porch, too big to be reined in by skin. That chiseled physique honed by hours of brutally challenging sports hadn't changed. A new scar stood out in sharp relief on his biceps, a long slash interlaced with crosshatches.

Stiches. Messy stitches, which meant he must have been sewn up by a third-world doctor after a zip-line accident in Off-The-Map City. Probably without anesthetic or antibiotics.

Still the same Shay.

She stepped back, refusing to dwell on scars—visible or otherwise—and nearly tripped over the Persian runner in the foyer. "Come in, please."

With another glance at the idling car, cryptic with its rental tags and tinted windows, he followed her into the house. Where to put him? In the living room or the less formal family room? She decided on formality, at least until she got her feet under her and her brain functional.

How could Shay still wreak such havoc on her senses after eight years?

Maybe because he was still gorgeous and untamed and… She didn't like that kind of man anymore, despite certain feminine parts trying to insist otherwise.

She ushered him into the living room and gestured to the plush navy couch. It was supposed to be big enough for two people but Shay's six-foot frame dwarfed it. As he settled onto a cushion, she worried for a fanciful second that the metal webbing beneath the fabric would collapse under the weight of so much man.

Eric was six feet tall. The couch had never seemed small when her ex-husband sat on it. She opted for the armless Queen Anne chair at a right angle to the couch and didn't allow a speck of self-analysis about why she hadn't sat next to Shay.

"I'm sorry about Grant and Donna," she said right away. The deaths of his friends and business partners was no doubt fresh on his mind. "How was the funeral?"

"Long." Grief welled inside his sea-glass-green eyes.

She could still see clear through them, straight into the wrenching agony of having to bury his best friends. Her primal, unchecked reaction to his emotions was frighteningly unchanged as well—a strong urge to soothe, to heal. To hold on to him until the pain fled.

Instead of reaching for him, she clasped her fingers together in a tight weave. They were virtually strangers now, no matter how abnormal it seemed. No matter how convinced she'd been that time would surely have dimmed the shimmering, irrational dynamic between them.

It hadn't. But she'd pretend it had.

Once, she'd been so drawn to his lust for life, to his powerful personality and his passion for everything—especially her—that he'd engulfed her, until she couldn't see the surface anymore. It was too much. *He* was too much.

She'd never been enough for him.

So why was he here? Instead of jumping right into it, she went with a safer subject. "Tell me about the funeral."

"We did both services together. Better that way, to get it all over with. Closed casket. It was easier. I didn't have to see them."

"Of course," she murmured. It wasn't like they'd had a choice.

Grant and Donna Greene had died in the explosion of an experimental ship designed for space tourism. News stations had continually replayed the clip, but Juliana couldn't imagine the couple being inside the craft when it blew. It was too ghastly. Instead, she remembered Shay's friends the way she'd last seen them eight years ago—standing on a bungee platform, sun beating down on the four of them as they waited to plunge into the unknown.

One by one, they'd jumped. First Shay, because he never failed to be first in line for whatever new thrill he'd conceived. Then Grant jumped, then Donna. They'd all jumped.

Except Juliana.

She couldn't—couldn't even peer over the edge. She'd just backed away with a wordless shake of her head, too overcome to speak. Too overwhelmed by the slippery darkness encroaching on her consciousness.

Shay was fearless. She wasn't. They didn't make sense together, and she'd known he'd eventually realize that, eventually grow bored with her at best, or resentful at worst.

She'd just realized the truth first.

She shook her head now and focused on the breathtaking mountains dominating the view through the floor-to-ceiling glass opposite her chair. She'd moved on, moved to New Mexico from Dallas for a reason. That hadn't been her place, in a relationship with a man who thrived on the indefinite, with whom she couldn't imagine a future. Or children. Or a normal marriage.

In New Mexico, she could find her balance in structure and order, the opposite of what her home life had been while growing up, the opposite of what she'd had with Shay. She could build a safe life firmly planted on the ground.

It just wasn't happening quite like she'd planned.

"How are you coping?" she asked. Her Dr. Cane voice betrayed nothing of the sharp and vivid memories fighting for her attention.

Eric disliked her Dr. Cane voice, disliked it when she answered all his questions with questions. Shay didn't seem at all bothered that she'd retreated behind her degree.

"Taking it day by day right now." Shay coughed and stared at the ceiling for a long time. "Greene, Greene and Shaylen has some good people running the show and that'll continue until I figure out some things."

"I'm so sorry, Shay. Let me get you a drink."

"First I have to tell you why I'm here. The will…" He cleared his throat. "Grant and Donna had a son. You probably heard. Their will named me as the guardian."

Her lungs contracted. That poor, motherless baby had been shuttled around with little regard, no doubt, for the potential trauma. Instinctively, she cupped her own barren womb and swallowed. "The news did mention a baby, but I assumed he went to relatives."

"I am a relative," Shay shot back. "Not by blood, but Grant was my brother in every way."

Juliana blinked at the fierceness clamping his mouth into a hard line. "Yes, I didn't mean anything by the term."

Shay backhanded a dark caramel-shot thatch of hair off his forehead. Almost every day of the two years they'd been together, he'd worn a baseball cap to keep that wavy mane out of his face. Had he traded the cap for something else or was he always bareheaded now?

"Sorry," he said. "It's been a hellacious couple of weeks. I'll get to the point. I'm a dad now. I owe Grant's kid the best shot at that I can give him. But I can't do it by myself. I need your help."

"My help? I haven't seen Grant and Donna since college."

Even then, they'd been part of Shay's world, not hers. The three were always together, poring over some complicated schematic. Muttering about accelerants and a myriad of other baffling rocket science terms. Three of the best minds in a generation hashing out improbable solutions for the optimal way to get off the ground. Always in a hurry to leave the earth—and Juliana—behind.

"You're a kid expert. That's what I need."

He'd been keeping tabs on her. Since she'd kept tabs on him, it shouldn't have come as a shock. Except Michael Shaylen's name graced the headlines every week, especially the past couple of years, once the cascade of government contracts awarded to GGS Aerospace catapulted its three founders onto the short list of billionaires under the age of thirty.

The story of her life was considerably less newsworthy. A dissertation arguing for more traditional child-rearing methods. Marriage to a compatible man. Four failed in vitro attempts. One quiet divorce and a year of floundering. But she was on track now, with a thriving psychology practice and the beginnings of a new parenting book. If she couldn't have a baby, she'd help other parents be the best they could be.

Much better than her own parents had ever been. They didn't know half of what had happened to her and didn't care to know. They'd always been too caught up in moving to the next town one step ahead of creditors to notice their daughter's problems, so she'd stopped telling them how rootless she'd felt. She'd stopped telling anyone.

All her angst, all her longing would be funneled into the book she'd conceptualized a few weeks ago. She'd birth a legacy instead of a baby.

"Yes, I'm a child psychologist. How does that make me what you need?"

"How do I raise him? How do I care for him?" Shay met her gaze and the strength of his plea hummed through the air. The years vanished as her flesh pebbled like it always had when provoked with that searing intensity. "Anyone can show me how to mix formula and change diapers. I'm asking you to teach me to be a father."

With a shiver, she ordered her goose bumps to cease and desist. He wanted her help, as a professional advisor of sorts. Not a smart idea. How could she work with him so closely when he still had such a strong effect on her? "That's a tall order. Hire a nanny."

"I plan to hire a nanny. Help me pick a good one. Help me pick schools, toys. Grant entrusted his son to me and I have to do everything right." The green tide pool of Shay's eyes sucked at her, mesmerizing her, as he pleaded his case.

He meant it.

Never would she have suspected such a sense of responsibility lurked in the heart of the roller coaster ride sprawled on her couch.

Eight years ago, she'd ended their relationship because she'd wanted to have children with a man who would raise them by her side, not one who was likely to wind up in a broken heap at the bottom of a cliff after his rappelling rope failed. Not one who willingly sought to upset the status quo every five seconds.

How ironic that *he* was the one who had ended up with the baby.

"Please, Juliana."

Shay fought the urge to clear his throat again.

He hadn't said her name aloud in a long time. Hadn't allowed himself to think about her. For the past eight years, he'd successfully avoided recalling what a mess she'd left behind when she'd walked out on him.

"Will you consider it? If the answer is no, I'll be on my way."

In the past twenty-four hours after making that phone call, he'd done nothing but think about Juliana Cane. The way her lips curled up in a half smile as she drew a bow across her violin. How she threw her head back while in the throes of pleasure. The exact shade of blue of her eyes.

Her still-gorgeous mouth pursed in thought, shifting the lines of her heartbreaker of a face. "What exactly are you proposing? I have clients. A practice. A life."

A life. Well, so did he. Or he used to. These days, life had an aggravating tendency to be one way when he woke up and a whole other way by the time his head hit the pillow that night. If he slept at all.

He hadn't closed his eyes once the night after Grant and Donna died. Too busy counting the if-onlys. Too busy shouldering blame and cursing himself for not double-checking that fuel line personally. Too busy figuring out that yeah, men weren't supposed to cry, but after losing everything that mattered, rules didn't apply.

Shay crossed his arms over the perpetual ache and scooted back against the fluffy, senior-citizen-approved couch cushions. "Sounds like the answer is yes."

She straightened the perfectly symmetrical hem to her grown-up suit and crossed her mile-long legs. "Yes to considering it. Iced tea? It's organic, and I only use stevia as a sweetener."

"Sure."

He hated iced tea and always had. What did it say that she didn't remember? Likely that she'd moved on and rightly so. They'd had no contact for eight years, and without the accident and his resulting parenthood, they would have continued to have no contact. Yeah, he'd followed her career. He couldn't help but wonder if she'd found the boring life she seemed to want.

Shay trailed Juliana into the neat kitchen, eyes on her heels. Nice. Did a lot for her already spectacular legs. Those legs dredged up crystal-clear memories of her smooth limbs wrapped around his waist, her hot torso heaving against his.

Their relationship had bordered on mythical. The sex had been awesome, too. Nearly a decade later, the heat between them was banked. But still there. He could feel it.

The kitchen told him a bunch about this new professional version of Juliana Cane. Canisters lined the immaculate counter, all labeled in precise script. No dishes in the sink, not even on a Saturday. Crayon drawings lined the refrigerator—the only visual difference between this kitchen and one set up in a pristine home décor showroom.

Seemed like she'd hit the boring jackpot. He'd hoped it would make her happy, but no one as passionate about music as Juliana had been would ever be happy with such a vanilla life. The sad lines around her mouth proved it.

"I'm proposing a job," he said as she retrieved a glass from an overhead cabinet. "In case that wasn't clear. A consulting gig. Name your price."

"Still not much of a negotiator, are you?"

She tucked a lock of pale blond hair behind her ear. A simple gesture, but a familiar one. Back in the day, Juliana's hair had always hung loose and sexy, curling along her shoulders, begging for a man's fingers to sweep it back.

His fingertips strained to reach for those pale locks but that wasn't the purpose of his visit. Mikey needed him. Juliana didn't.

"Negotiation is for people who can afford to walk away if the terms aren't agreeable. I'm not trying to bargain. If I had another choice, I'd take it. You're the last person I expected to be asking for help."

The iced tea she'd been pouring splattered on the counter, missing the glass by six inches.

Rattled. Good. He barely recognized the woman she'd grown into. She looked the same, made some of the same gestures, but her reserve bothered him. He wasn't sure what he'd been expecting, but it wasn't this polite stranger.

With the baby's welfare sitting like bricks on his shoulders, the last thing he should be thinking about was how to rattle Juliana some more. But he was.

"I see." She wiped up the spilled tea without looking at him. "It seems we have some latent issues to address before we can enter a consulting arrangement."

No. There was no way he was discussing what had happened in college. He grinned, the best form of deflection he had on him. "The past is the past. Let's leave it there. Now it's addressed. Name your price."

She handed him the glass, blank-faced. "I'd hardly call that addressing it. But I'm willing to let it lie, at least until I decide if I'll accept. There's a lot to consider."

Calling her had dug up difficult memories, but he owed Grant and Donna. Mikey deserved the best. Shay wasn't leaving without Juliana's agreement. "Allow me to play the sympathy card, then. Be right back."

He left Juliana and the glass of revolting tea in the kitchen and let himself out the front door. He waved at the car and Linda stepped out with Mikey fast asleep in her arms. His admin carried the baby to Juliana's porch. Gingerly, Shay took him. Such a little guy to have so much expectation attached to him, and no matter what anyone said, holding him was nothing like carrying a football.

Linda held the door open and retreated to the car. He'd really stretched her job description lately and the raise he'd already given her wasn't nearly enough. If he could get Juliana's help, his admin was due for a two-week, all-expenses-paid cruise.

As soon as he cleared the foyer, Juliana came out of the kitchen.

"Oh." Juliana's hand flew to her mouth. "I didn't know you brought him."

"Figured you could say no to me, but not to that face." He grinned at the quiet baby. First time in God knew how long Mikey wasn't screaming his head off. "This guy here is Michael Grant Greene. We call him Mikey."

Juliana's eyes filled. "They named him after you."

It wasn't a question but he nodded, his throat too tight to respond. That had pretty much been the way of things for two weeks. Lots of nodding. Lots of pretending that if he could run a billion-dollar company, raising a baby should be a snap. But Mikey wasn't just a baby. Mikey was his kid now. He'd already started adoption proceedings.

Why hadn't someone warned him a piece of paper didn't automatically bestow parenting powers? He was doing what he always did—facing down the gaping jaws of challenge without blinking. So why wasn't he getting to a place where it started to come together, where the thick coating of scared-out-of-his-mind didn't strangle him twenty-four hours a day?

The sleek blonde peering at him from those earthy blue eyes was going to get him back on solid ground. She'd always had a way about her, as if she could carry the world on her shoulders without stumbling. Steadiness. He'd missed that.

Missed her.

Where had that come from?

The past was in the past, but it hadn't been a very clean break. He'd done a lot of yelling and Juliana had cried a lot but ultimately, she stubbornly dug her toes into the ground and he craved the sky. Both of them had been unwilling to compromise.

He'd loved her. A lot. But not enough to take up knitting so she'd have a guarantee he'd be in one piece at the end of the day. So she'd dumped him because she couldn't love him as is. He was an adrenaline junkie to the core, sure, but he'd channeled considerable energy into their relationship. Some women would have sacrificed limbs to be so fiercely loved. It still stung that she wasn't one of them.

If he'd known being in her presence would stir all that up again, he'd never have picked up the phone.

Their voices—or whatever demons haunted the baby— woke Mikey and he let loose with a shriek. *That* was the kid he'd lived with for the past two weeks. Shay rocked his arms. "Shh. Shh."

Stupid soothing noises never worked but neither did anything else.

"Let me." Juliana gathered up the baby, her eyes lit from within as she focused on the bundle of blanket and bleating kid, and nestled him against her breast. Mikey buried his face in her shirt and miraculously shut up.

Humming. Juliana was humming. He'd never thought of that.

Early-morning floor-treading, night after night, gave birth to much insanity and calling Juliana obviously topped the list. But usually nothing worked to stop Mikey's constant crying. Shay was at the end of his rope. Mikey needed more than what Shay could physically do, and late at night, all he could think about was how Juliana had once made everything all right.

"See?" Shay whispered. "That's why I'm here. You're perfect for this job. Say yes."

The tremulous smile on her face sent a shaft of hope through him. Hope and warmth. Eight years was a long time. They'd both changed—Juliana clearly more so, with her professional reserve and grown-up clothes—but regardless, he'd spent a long time not thinking about her. How hard could it be to work together?

"Fifty thousand dollars. And I want to write a book about it. You agree to let me use the experience, and I'll do it."

Did she not know how much he was worth? He'd have paid

a million without hesitation. "A book? Diapers and giraffe mobiles aren't a very interesting story. Maybe you should add a vampire."

"Non-fiction. About parenting." She shifted Mikey higher on her chest and brushed her lips across his baby-fine hair with a tiny smile. "It's a project I've been thinking about for a while and I need a good platform. Teaching a man to be a father is great in and of itself. The fact that it's you will make it a bestseller."

"You want to use my name in a book?" A half step away from selling the story to a tabloid, and partly the reason why he was here instead of interviewing someone from Nannies-R-Us. "That's going a little far."

"You asked my price. I'm not the one with the problem."

Apparently it *was* a negotiation. One day, he'd learn to think before speaking. Before it was too late to take back his words. "Only if I get approval of the final version and you stay at my house so you can be on call all the time. That's *my* price."

Looked like today wasn't the day he'd learn his lesson because he definitely could have thought of a better way to phrase that. He hadn't meant *that* kind of on call. But now he was thinking about it. A beautiful, single woman would be in his house, eating, sleeping—did she still sleep naked?

Her expression blanked. "I'd prefer to do it via video conferencing. Virtual consulting is as good as in person."

"Not to me. I want total immersion. Mikey responds to you. I barely know how to change diapers and I have no idea what else I don't know. I want to be a dad who puts Band-Aids on his knee and throws a ball in the backyard. That doesn't happen automatically."

Not even when the dad shared DNA with his son. Shay's own father had never done Band-Aids or ball-throwing. The first time Shay had picked up Mikey after being awarded custody, he knew instantly he would be a different kind of dad, the kind he'd always wanted. The best replacement dad he could be. He had every intention of living up to the confidence Grant had in him.

Softness stole across her mouth. "No. It doesn't. It takes commitment and sacrifice and it starts in the cradle. Some parents don't understand that. It says a lot that you do."

"Thanks." He shrugged, unsure why the compliment meant so much. "Will you do it?"

"What's the time frame? The breadth of fatherhood is a lot to cover in a week."

"Then stay for six months. A year. I'll double the money."

She shook her head and frowned. "I can't leave my practice that long. Some of these kids are really damaged. They need me."

"They can get another therapist. I can't get another you."

Their gazes crashed and she held him captive, drawing out a connection that pulled him in like a magnet. She felt it, too—he could see the sway of her shoulders. Was she remembering how good it had been? The idea fed his own memory, and he couldn't shut off the video in his head.

He'd moved on because he'd had no choice. Didn't mean he'd forgotten the curves now hiding under her prim suit or the way she kept a good hold on him as she blasted him into outer space. The way she'd been the only one he'd wanted waiting for him when he came back to Earth.

"Perhaps we should discuss the nature of the arrangement you're offering." Her dry tone left no doubt she'd been right there with him on the trip down memory lane. "It's strictly professional or no deal."

He'd also never forgotten what had happened after he'd broken his leg snowboarding. She'd said sayonara and left his heart in pieces that never fit back together quite the same way. There was no worse pain than being told you weren't okay exactly the way you were. Her love was conditional, available only if he became someone else, someone safe and acceptable.

He could hire a nanny tomorrow. Ask his mom for advice. But he wanted the best and he'd pay the emotional price for it.

"Of course. I'm interested in you for your expertise," he said, but it was only half the truth.

He was also, suddenly, perversely, interested in proving to Juliana she'd made a big mistake by walking out on him. In proving he could get under the skin of this buttoned-up Juliana who was clearly willing to ignore the humming vibe between them. By the time he was through, she wouldn't be ignoring anything. And she'd admit she wanted him. As is.

"I'll help you," she said, leaving him rabidly curious about why she'd agreed. Because of Mikey, the book or that trip down memory lane? He'd never been able to read her and the mystery intrigued him. "For a couple of months. I have to make arrangements for my clients and it'll take a week or so. I'd like to see each of them personally to explain my absence."

It was done. Relief flooded that empty place hollowed out by the explosion. The most qualified consultant money could buy would help him become the father Mikey deserved. If he was smart, he'd leave it at that.

He'd rather rattle Dr. Cane than play it safe.

Two

Two months. She should have her head examined.

The baby had won her over and Juliana wasn't ashamed to admit Shay had played her like a maestro. How had he known Mikey's sweet face would be the clincher? Lucky guess? Calculated offensive?

Either way, here she was in West Texas, descending a set of metal stairs locked to the hatch of a GGS Aerospace jet, a mere five days after Shay had showed up on her doorstep. Fate and a great assistant had seen to fitting all fifteen of her clients into a two-day block, and then she'd had no more excuses.

What was it about Shay's proposal that set her on edge like the screech of an out-of-tune string?

The book deal would make this experience well worth her while. The yearning to nurture flowed through her veins, sometimes so fast and thick she feared they would burst, and she couldn't let all that love for babies go to waste. She wanted to share everything she'd learned.

The money would be welcome, too. Half a year's salary for two months' work was highway robbery but Shay hadn't fluttered an eyelid at the figure. In vitro procedures and student loans for a PhD certainly did not come cheaply, and she'd appreciate a faster decline in her debt.

So why did it feel like the bottom would drop out from under her at any moment?

A low-slung maroon Acura sat on the tarmac a healthy distance from the plane. Shay leaned against the rear end, his hip resting against the car casually, arms crossed. Today he'd opted for the trademark ball cap. Backward, as always.

So he did still wear caps. The sight threw her back in time for a moment, reminding her of when she'd mostly seen him without it. In bed.

She shuddered and willed away the punch to her abdomen.

He was one big chunk of vibrant, testosterone-filled man. So not her type. A younger and stupider Juliana had thrown caution to the wind, ignoring how incompatible they were, reveling in the wild buzz of his no-holds-barred approach to everything. She'd never do that again.

"You have Tony Stark's car?" she asked by way of greeting. "And they let you drive it onto the runway?"

"Comes with owning the runway." He grinned that whole-face grin she'd never been able to take her eyes off of. "I bought my NSX before *The Avengers* came out, by the way. How do you know what kind of car Tony Stark drives?"

"Three of my clients are teenagers. Girls with movie-star crushes." Gritty wind blew across the open space of GGS Aerospace, stinging her skin with its sandy teeth. "So is this where all the magic happens?"

"Some. There's a hangar around back for the jet and the office is about a half mile away." He nodded to the sleek glass-and-marble building at the edge of the tarmac. "This will eventually be the commercial hub once we get the space tourism division up and running. Once *I* get it running."

Stylish sunglasses hid his eyes but the catch in his voice said he still hadn't fully internalized the loss of his partners. Or, likely, what he'd gained. Some people would feel incredibly blessed to be given a child. Did he? Or was it a responsibility he'd accepted, but would never see as more than that?

"GGS is largely a military aircraft supplier," he continued after a minute of heavy silence. "The manufacturing division is outside of Fort Worth and we have a high-rise in downtown for operations. I go back and forth by helicopter. Land's cheaper out here and you need a lot of it to run a space tourist business."

"Uh-huh." She wasn't here to learn the ins and outs of a company that designed and built the most dangerous flying machines known to man. She and Shay weren't old friends catching up over a casual conversation. He was a client, and she had a job to do. "I assume your house is close by?"

"A couple of miles. Ready?" Shay grabbed two of the three suitcases the crew had deposited on the concrete and tilted his head to the remaining one. With his arms uncrossed, she could read his shirt—My Parents Were Abducted by Aliens and All I Got Was This Lousy T-shirt.

As if she needed additional clues that he was still mentally fourteen. Shay's Peter Pan syndrome had been part of his charm, part of the reason she hadn't brushed him off when he'd called out to her at the library that fateful day in September when they'd first met. She'd feared then that he'd never grow up and hated discovering she'd been right.

Success and newly acquired wealth had clearly afforded him a bigger playground for his dangerous toys instead of instilling a good dose of reality. People depended on him, more so now than ever. What would they do if he got seriously hurt? If he died?

The less she dwelled on that, the better. She had only one responsibility here, and Shay wasn't it.

She hefted the suitcase into the car and sank into the

leather passenger seat. The dash sported a variety of gizmos and dials well suited for a driver who liked to know every last statistic of an engine's performance.

Shay stomped the accelerator and hit Mach 1 in about a minute. She resisted the urge to grab something and bit back the "slow down" fighting to be voiced.

"Tell me more about Mikey," she said instead over the wail of strings piping from the speakers.

Classical music and Shay seemed incongruous—until she remembered how he'd come to her performances, front row center for every one. How he'd told her so many times what a thrill it was to watch her play the violin. He'd endured it for her—or so she'd assumed. In hindsight, it seemed he'd just liked the music.

"He's a baby. What else is there?"

The flat, ugly landscape flew by, barely allowing her to register the dotting of cacti. Shay's hands were solid on the wheel, in full command of the machine under them.

"A lot. How old is he? Start there and we'll get to all of it eventually."

Watching his curled hands set off a hot flush in her long-forgotten places. Mortified, she jerked her head toward the window and focused on the mountains. She wasn't twenty-two anymore and over the years sex had become a utilitarian mechanism necessary for pregnancy. Now it was unnecessary entirely.

"Almost six months. I think. Maybe five."

"I need to know exactly. Babies start on solid food at six months. He should already be on rice cereal."

"My conversations with Donna started and ended with engines."

Not a surprise. Juliana remembered Donna as someone more likely to recite a complicated equation than the date her son had first rolled over. Motherhood might have changed Mikey's mother, but Juliana doubted it. After all, what kind of mother got into an experimental spaceship without any regard to the potential consequences? Like leaving her baby to the adrenaline junkie behind the wheel of a car suited for a superhero.

"She never talked about her child? What about Grant?"

"They talked about him all the time. I didn't pay a whole lot of attention, I guess. When they talked about a breakthrough on the liquid oxygen alternative, that's when I tuned in. It's weird to think about Donna as a mother instead of an engineer. The failed prototype was Donna's. She designed it from the ground up. Worked on it for three years."

That explained a lot. "Sometime today, call Mikey's pediatrician. I'll give you a list of things to ask."

"Uh, okay."

Juliana sighed. "Call Donna's admin and get the name and number from her. Then start taking notes. If you want to be a father, then you have to know these things. What would you have done if Mikey developed a fever?"

"Called Linda. *My* admin," he clarified before she could ask. "I must not have been clear back at your house. I need help. Not judgment."

She unclenched her teeth. "I'm sorry."

Shay needed her on his side. Knowing how to care for a child wasn't innate, not even for females. Her own mother wouldn't have won any awards; in fact, she'd thoroughly failed at instilling a sense of security in her daughter, the most important aspect of childrearing.

Most women—women who were interested—used all nine months to learn everything they could, breathing baby books until their water broke. Shay would have to do it in eight weeks and without benefit of a highly motivating nesting instinct.

He was trying. She should be trying, too, not jumping down his throat because he was still outrageously sexy and she'd just received the very nasty wake-up call that she wasn't immune to it. She had to find an inoculation quickly because she wasn't leaving this job without solid notes for her book and she wasn't falling back into Shay's crazy.

"We're here."

Shay hit a button on the visor and the wrought-iron gate connecting a stone wall swung open. He drove onto the property, and she got her first glimpse of a billionaire's life.

"What are all those cranes for around the lake?" she asked and noted they were connected to a wire line circling the water.

"It's a wakeboard cable system. You should try it while you're here. I've already called my architect to come enclose the lake and the outdoor pool with something a kid can't get through. Made his year with the dollar signs I waved under his nose."

See, she assured herself, Shay wasn't completely clueless. That meant her job wouldn't be as difficult as she'd envisioned.

The house—a term which could only be applied in the loosest sense to the enormous glass-and-steel structure—straddled the center of the estate, unfolding in both directions with multiple floors, balconies and sharp rooflines. "All this for one person?"

"Eight people," he corrected immediately. "Me, Mikey and the staff."

Not a house. A home. He and Mikey would be a family. A sharp spike behind her rib cage reminded her she'd left Shay to find a stable man who could give her a stable life, complete with children, and now she'd be creating exactly that with Shay after all.

Only she'd have to walk away in a few short weeks, leaving a gap wide open for someone else to slide into.

"You said outdoor pool. There's an indoor pool, too? Never mind. I have plenty of time to acquaint myself with all the goodies." Private jets, indoor pools and an extreme athlete's body she'd been very careful not to notice. She almost offered him an aspirin for the sore arm he must have from beating off the women with a stick. "I'm not here to act as your glorified babysitter while you jet off to Paris with this week's playmate, am I?"

She'd assumed when they'd split that he'd find a girl better suited to being flung off a cliff—emotional and actual—but his love life after her had always been a nebulous, murky idea. Now it was real and she swallowed against the sudden burn in her throat.

He shot her a sideways scowl and threw the car into Park. "Yeah, I've got dates lined up out the door. A different woman every night while Mikey cries himself to sleep. My social life is nonexistent. Thanks for the reminder."

He barreled out of the car. When he opened her door, she stepped out onto the stained concrete circular drive and grabbed his hand before he could turn away. Something needed to change but she wasn't sure what. She hated being unsure.

"Should I scrawl 'I'm sorry' across my forehead with a Sharpie? I'm bound to get laryngitis as many times as I've had to say it."

He chuckled and it spread through her abdomen with a tingle.

"How about a truce instead?" He flipped her hand and shook it. "We used to get along pretty well. Let's see if we can find a way back to that."

The weight of his fingers against hers took on a whole new meaning. "That sounds suspiciously like the opposite of professional."

"Hmm, you think so?" His hand tightened and a thumb brushed over her knuckle in a long stroke. The sparks submerged her senses with the kind of quick heat she'd done her best to forget, but it came rushing back in a torrent of memory.

"Uh-huh. The opposite."

"You said that already."

He was watching her with intense, impossible-to-look-away-from focus, leaning into her, a slight tilt away from something irreversible. Crazy. Dangerous and frightening.

"We should go inside," she rasped and cleared her throat, breaking the connection and sweeping her hair off her shoulders in a poor attempt to reorient, which surely didn't fool Shay. "Will you show me to my room?"

"Sure. I'll send someone out for your bags."

No catch in *his* voice, because she'd never affected him the way he did her, as if her legs would collapse at any moment. Firm, solid ground, that's what she needed.

He mounted the patterned steps lined with twenty-foot palm trees and exotic flowers that shouldn't grow in the desert but did because they belonged to Shay. He created magic from nothing, an alchemy she'd never been able to analyze until it made sense.

She reminded herself that she didn't need to understand him. She only needed to do her job, get research notes for her book and get out.

Forty-seven hallways later, her head spun from trying to take in the luxurious room Shay had ushered her into. The four-poster bed presided over the room from a raised dais, leading to an inviting seating area to the left that shared a flat-screen TV mounted on a swivel arm between them.

One whole wall was clear acrylic, enclosing a tank full of colorful, darting fish, coral and glowing anemones. The remaining walls were painted a purple so dark, it should have closed in the space, but actually worked well to unite the separate areas. Raw silk in lighter purples, off-white and black covered the bed and was repeated in the fabrics of the seating area and window treatments.

It was difficult to reconcile all this wealth and opulence with the rough-around-the-edges man she'd known in college. "Your home is beautiful."

"My mom." He twisted his mouth into a self-deprecating grin. "She and the decorator were texting each other within two days. I figured why ruin her fun? So I let her have free rein."

Juliana recalled Mrs. Shaylen being a very proper, nervous woman who taught English at a private high school in Dallas. They'd never gotten along well, though Juliana couldn't fathom why not. They shared a strong desire to see Shay live until his next birthday and he'd ignored both of them equally well.

"I'll unpack later. We should start right away with Mikey. What does he usually do in the afternoons?"

"Different stuff. I temporarily reassigned one of the maids to Mikey. Maria. She raised five kids but has no interest in long-term child care. He's with her now. She watches him if I have to go into the office or do a conference call from home."

"Maybe that's where we should start. What are the next two months going to look like? What are you hoping to accomplish? Total immersion means there won't be a lot of going into the office. We should organize a list of goals and then assign blocks of time to—"

"Whoa, Schedule Police. Is all that necessary?"

"Yes, extremely. We have a limited amount of time and a lot to cover. We need a plan of attack. Additionally, it's important to note children thrive on schedules. They like to know what's coming next. It's comforting. Schedules are now a part of your life."

In the time she'd taken to explain the most fundamental concept Shay needed to learn, he'd edged into her space. The fine lines he'd grown around his eyes were deeper than she'd realized, aging him. He wasn't twenty-two anymore, either, and it fit him nicely.

If only the inside had aged as well as the outside.

"Hey, Ju?" His gaze flitted over her and the atmosphere tangibly shifted, growing dense and tight. "Danged if I don't like this new you. That high-brow tone you get when you're being all consulty-like, it's really sexy."

She narrowed an eye at him. "Say what?"

"Yeah. I like it. Give me some more." His cheekbones drew upward as he smiled wolfishly.

"Um." Now she had a really keen awareness of exactly how close Shay was and exactly how far away the door was. The clean freshness of his soap frayed her senses. It wasn't what he used to smell like. "That was all I had to say."

"Too bad. What should we do now?"

"Unpack." Hadn't she just said she could do that later? She took a step backward, hoping the movement would jar her brain into functioning again. "Then we can go over some basics."

"Or," he said, wrapping his tongue around the *r* in a thoroughly suggestive way, "I could put some Shay in your sway, baby."

Her eyes shut for a brief, insane second. The first time he'd laid that line on her, she'd laughed and let him take her to dinner. After an appropriate period of dating, he'd sweet-talked her clothes off and she'd spent forty-eight hours in his bed losing all sense of time and place. His full-on masculine quicksand had sucked her under and kept her there. Pulling free had been the hardest thing she'd ever done.

"My sway is A-Okay, thanks." Dr. Seuss instead of Dr. Cane. Shay yanked her out of academia, yanked her out of reasonableness. He had to stop. "We agreed it was best to have a professional association only."

When he reached out and fingered a lock of hair, she almost jerked out of her skin. With a perplexed once-over, he dropped his hand, allowing her to breathe again.

"No. I said I was hiring you for your expertise. I did not agree to the distance between us. Feels wrong. That line worked once to get your attention. Figured I'd try it again."

Distance. She wished she didn't know precisely what he

meant. In college, they'd talked about everything, joked and flirted without censor. There was a strange edge now that cut in ways she hadn't anticipated. "Well, I'm not falling for it again."

"Maybe I'll find a different line, then." When she cocked a brow, he shrugged and said, "It's weird to be dancing around our past, trying to avoid land mines."

"So you figured you'd step on one deliberately?"

"Hey, it's easier to deal with an explosion you know is coming than one you don't."

Shay's straightforward approach was a far cry from text-book psychology and he seldom followed conventions any-way. Her doctorate wouldn't get much traction here and they *did* have to spend time together. "Let's ditch the explosives and try something else, like really putting the past behind us. We're different people now. Maybe this time around, we can be friends."

His grin could have melted butter. "Can we have a sleepover and watch scary movies? I haven't had a good mid-night pillow fight in ages."

She laughed. "Sorry, sport. Your future includes diapers and bottles. But I'll gladly stay up late with you for that."

The pages of Shay's life were turning so fast, he barely had time to read the words, let alone absorb them. If every-thing slowed down, he might catch up.

He should be asleep. Instead, he was watching the digital clock. Mikey woke up between one-fifteen and one-twenty pretty much every night, like the kid's stomach had an alarm. Shay usually woke in cold panic right before the witching hour, terrified he'd missed the opening wail, effectively forc-ing a helpless baby to lie there crying while Shay slept.

The video monitor on Shay's nightstand showed an immo-bile lump in the middle of the crib. On cue, the lump stirred and let out a yowl. Shay hit the carpet and threw on a shirt before trudging to the connecting door between his bedroom and Mikey's. He wanted to bond with Mikey and this was part of it, but some nights he wished they could bond through the mutual act of sleep.

"Shh. I'm here." He scooped up the baby and gathered him against a shoulder. He carried the mewling bundle to the kitchenette he'd paid double to have installed in the corner of the nursery within twenty-four hours of the reading of the will. Murmuring nonsense words, he went through the rote motions of heating water and mixing formula for the hungry bottomless pit snuffling against his shirt.

A whiff of female filtered in underneath the strong sour of formula.

"Hey," Juliana whispered behind him.

Every nerve lit up as if he'd crested a mountain in his Cessna and an endless valley fell away under the wings. It'd be nice to blame his reaction on lack of sex. Or sleep. But he'd gone without both many times and it had never caused spontaneous bursts of poetry and awareness.

She thought they should try to be friends. Screw that. She'd have to get used to the idea that he wanted her in his arms, naked and shuddering with pleasure.

He grabbed the full bottle and shot her a smile over his shoulder. "Welcome to my world."

She smiled back, tousled and gorgeous in her just-out-of-bed state. "Can I feed him?"

"Is the dark side of the moon cold?"

One eyebrow crinkled. "I'll take that as a yes."

He waited until she settled into the rocking chair and positioned the baby against her thighs, his fingertips tingling where he'd brushed her. The kid went after the bottle like an alcoholic with a fifth of Jim Beam.

Shay slumped against the wall and slid to the carpet. Tomorrow he'd order another chair. Should have already done that. It hadn't registered there'd be two people in the nursery taking care of Mikey at the same time.

In record time, Mikey drained the bottle. She set the empty bottle on the low table beside the rocking chair and lifted Mikey up to burp him. Here came the really fun part.

Mikey cried. And cried. No matter what Juliana did, he cried more. Worry lines popped up around her eyes as she patted and rubbed Mikey's back.

"Yeah, you might as well settle in and get comfortable," he advised. "He'll do that for about another hour."

"Shay, that's not normal. How many days has he cried more than a few minutes after eating?"

"All of them. Babies cry a lot, don't they?" Unease trickled across his shoulders. Was something wrong with Mikey and he'd been too clueless to connect the dots?

Juliana shot off a round of questions, which he did his best to answer. If nothing else, he'd found the right person to help—she was something, asking things he'd never have considered, like if he'd spoken to Donna's nanny about whether Donna used a different brand of formula or if she'd been breastfeeding. Yeah, that was a conversation he was dying to have. He scrubbed at his jaw, bristling the short hairs sideways. What kind of dad balked at saying *breastfeeding* out loud?

"He probably has reflux. We'll get it fixed, won't we, honey?" she murmured in Mikey's ear and started humming, rocking the chair simultaneously. When that didn't work, she laid him across her knees, facedown and rubbed his back.

"How do you know to do all these things? Your grad school professors must have loved you." His professors had hated him, as they tended to when a student could ace a test without reading the textbook or showing up for lectures. Mind-numbing stuff. He and Grant had dropped out of MIT's graduate program and started GGS Aerospace while Donna finished her PhD. Best move he'd ever made.

Second best had been hiring Juliana to turn him into a father. She was doing exactly what he'd hoped—making everything all right.

She stood and walked with Mikey, pacing around the nursery with swaying steps. Mikey was slung over her shoulder, head hanging down her back. Finally, he burped and quieted down.

"I didn't learn about babies in grad school," she said once she'd wrapped Mikey up in the blankets mummy-style. But when she didn't elaborate, his curiosity was piqued. They'd split in their senior year at SMU and she'd had eight years' worth of life since then.

"Watch a lot of baby videos online?" That's what he'd done. Learned enough to get by and enough to know he needed far more help than five-minute snippets posted by internet wannabe-stars.

"I read a few books." Mikey was nestled in her arms peacefully and she kept her eyes on the baby, then busied herself with placing him back in the crib.

Shay crossed his fingers. Sometimes the baby went to sleep and sometimes, the second he hit the mattress, he started screaming again. Tonight was a back-to-sleep night. Thank God.

Shay's already lit-up nerves weren't faring well with the dual punch of Juliana and screaming baby.

They tiptoed out of the nursery, parting to retreat to their separate bedrooms. And met again inside the nursery at 4:05 a.m., the second hour engrained in Mikey's stomach.

Bleary-eyed, Juliana shuffled a step closer. "He's still waking up twice a night?"

"That's not normal, either?"

Man, was anything about this kid right? Genetically speaking, he should be well ahead of the curve. Maybe it was Shay's fault—corrupting the baby with his lack of experience.

When he moved toward the crib, she tugged him back with a hand to his elbow. "We'll let the baby cry it out this time."

Let the baby cry on *purpose?* He eyed the bawling lump and then eyed Juliana. She nodded toward the door and left. Mystified, he followed her back into his bedroom, Mikey's wails grating down his spine.

"We'll watch him for a while." Juliana sank onto the bed between his pillow and kicked-away sheets and motioned to the monitor.

Her face glowed in the pale moonlight spilling from the window opposite the bed. Middle of the night, yet in tailored pajamas and robe, she exuded classiness.

If he'd known a woman would be in his bed, he might have requested silk sheets. What a flat-out disgrace it wasn't that kind of late-night party. He snapped on the bedside light. No point in maintaining ambiance.

As he moved away from the bed, his toes curled against the hardwood floor. It was cold, but the carpet only stuck out about a foot around the bed frame. With all the *hands-off* Dr. Cane had been throwing around, it seemed like he should keep a respectable distance from the consultant in his bed.

At least until he figured out how to bridge it.

"All these books you read to learn about babies. You read those recently?" he asked.

The whole concept of ignoring a crying baby stuck in his craw. If something needed attention, you handled it. But he was paying for expert advice. How much sense did it make to second-guess the doctor?

"In the last few years," she said.

"So, not as preparation for this job."

"I reread some on the plane. You hired me to teach you to be a father. Caring for a baby is part of that but it's not my primary field of expertise. Child-rearing as a whole is."

"I know." Mikey was still sobbing with no signs of stopping. Every muscle in Shay's body stood tensed, ready to spring toward the door, but she remained calm, grounded. He'd missed having ready access to that strength. "I read your dissertation."

Juliana jerked her gaze away from the monitor to stare at him. "You did? All of it?"

"You think I called you up for old times' sake? I did my research."

"I'm just surprised. It's dry, pure academics. Most people would fall asleep after two paragraphs."

"I didn't. You wrote it. I was always fascinated by your mind."

She processed that, blank-faced. While he often blurted out exactly what was on his mind without restriction, she spoke very carefully, then and now. "You can't still find me interesting."

"Yet I do." And he grew more interested by the minute.

She'd always turned him on but this grown-up version of Juliana was something else. A challenge and a half. What was it going to take to break through her resolve to keep things professional between them?

The only way to find out was to rattle her some more and see what was what.

They stared at each other for a long time and he realized his muscles had relaxed. Mikey was still crying but intermittently. The restless urge to move had stabilized and for the first time since the explosion, he didn't want to go climb something or fly something or jump off something to beat back the weight of life.

"Hey, Ju, do you still play the violin?" The question flew from his mouth in hopes of keeping her in his bed for a while longer. He wanted to talk some more. And he liked the view.

"No. I haven't played since college."

The forlorn note in her voice tightened his chest. He'd loved listening to her play with the campus chamber group, could still see her in his mind, bow raised, her elation flying through the air with the notes. "You were good. Why did you quit?"

She shrugged. "Busy. It's hard to take time for something frivolous when you have so much going on."

Somehow he'd moved toward the bed, knees bumping the mattress. Since he was already here, he might as well sit. "But you loved playing. If you love it, it's not frivolous."

No wonder she seemed so unhappy—she'd stopped letting the music feed her soul.

With a wry smile, she lay back against his pillow and a flash of memory overlaid the present—one of her reclined exactly like that, but naked, eyes hot with anticipation as she waited for him.

"Says the man who builds spaceships in his spare time. Not everyone gets to do whatever they want with their life."

And with that bucket of cold water, the memory extinguished. Yes, he was lucky to get to follow his passion. A passion that had killed the most important people in his life. Juliana had once been on that list and all of a sudden, the list felt really blank.

"What would you be if you could be anything?"

"A mom," she said softly. "Not in the cards."

"Your ex didn't want children?"

He shifted, brushing a hand across her leg accidentally-on-purpose. She jolted as if she'd taken a slug to the torso.

"You knew I'd been married?"

After she'd agreed to help him, a discreet P.I. out of Dallas had done exhaustive research on her and Eric Whittaker, the accountant she'd been married to for three years. "I came across it."

Her ex was a dweeb with vacant eyes, who'd obviously sucked in bed if Shay's casual touch caused such a visible reaction. If Mikey took a few days to adjust, this late-night-rendezvous deal might work in his favor. He could do some more rattling. A hot and thick flood drained into his lower half at the thought of the reaction he might get with a few better-placed touches.

She sighed with a heavy lift of her chest. "He wanted children. We tried the natural way, then the artificial way. Science isn't good enough to overcome the defects of nature."

"I'm sorry. That's when you read all those baby books, isn't it?" Her tight nod said everything she didn't. "Is it hard to be here, with Mikey?"

Surprise flitted across her face. "I'm a professional. I'll do my job."

"Hey." He leaned forward and took her hand. She'd extended the olive branch of friendship and he'd done nowhere near enough to pick it up. Of course, he didn't intend to stop there, but it was a good start. "I'm asking because you interest me. Not because I think you'll shirk your responsibilities."

Some pretty major stuff had happened in her life. Rattling his way past the professional barrier she'd erected was going to be harder than he'd expected. But he'd find a way.

She looked down at their joined fingers and faked a yawn. "Mikey's asleep. Good night."

Then she slipped away.

Three

Mikey's pediatrician diagnosed him with reflux, as Juliana had suspected he would. Funny how being right did little to boost her energy or her mood. Cry-it-out had only worked the first night. A week later, the reflux medicine and several different kinds of formula hadn't worked at all. Since Maria worked only during the day and Shay hadn't specified his nanny requirements, they split nighttime baby duty.

Fuzzily, she peered at the hands of the elephant clock on the nursery wall. 5:00 a.m. or 5:00 p.m.? A glance at the dark window answered the question. Did it matter? Time ceased to have any meaning when on call every day. She patted the screaming bundle of baby propped up on her shoulder. He'd been crying for nearly an hour.

How had Donna done this, over and over, and still functioned?

Regardless of whose turn it was, Mikey never smiled, or gurgled or did any cute baby things. Regardless of who claimed to be an expert, the result was the same. Failure.

Wiggling baby woke her. She blinked hair out of her eyes and sucked in a breath at the stab of pain through her neck and shoulders. Daylight poured through the nursery window, washing over the cartoon giraffes, lions, hippos and zebras painted on the walls. Mikey peered up at her from a nest of blankets across her thighs, uncharacteristically quiet.

She'd fallen asleep in the rocking chair with an unsecured five-month-old baby on her lap. He could have rolled off or she might have flipped him off accidentally. His head could have gotten stuck between the cushions.

His mother would never have been so irresponsible.

Of course, no matter how much she'd come to care about Mikey, Juliana was just a consultant. One who couldn't get her brain jump-started when around the baby's father.

The connecting door between Shay's room and the nursery opened. Shay buzzed through and in the split second before he shut it, the door frame outlined Shay's bed.

His mattress was soft and fluffy, with warm, inviting sheets, and she'd been very careful not to think about it. That first night, they'd been talking and it had been so familiar she hadn't thought twice about sitting on his bed. Until he started looking at her with those Shay eyes, as if her respectable tailored pajamas and robe were transparent and he liked what they revealed.

There went that hot flush in a place that had no business flushing. Knowing his way around a woman's body didn't begin to compensate for lack of maturity and addiction to danger. Her well-educated brain shouldn't have so much trouble remembering.

"Hey, Ju," he said. "Did you get some sleep?"

"A little." She clutched Mikey against her chest. He needed her, and it was her job to keep him safe. "I dozed off in the rocker."

What a waste of a degree. What did she know about child rearing? A bunch of rhetoric from textbooks. The real thing kept kicking her in the teeth, minute by minute. How many parents had she sanctimoniously lectured about their mistakes, as they nervously perched on their seats in her office? How had not one of them denounced her as a fraud?

Yet she arrogantly presumed to write a book about this.

He nodded. "Been there many a time, my friend."

"Well, it's not advisable. We can't keep up this middle-of-the-night marathon. Today, we need to figure out the nanny plan."

With a nanny in place, Juliana would have distance from day-to-day care and regain her professional perspective. Then maybe she'd figure out how best to care for him. He was depending on her.

"I have a better idea. You need a break. I have a few things to take care of in Fort Worth this morning. Come with me. You can go shopping and I'll take you to lunch. Maria will watch Mikey and we'll be back by two or three at the latest."

A break? If he'd said Godiva chocolate dipped in twenty-four-karat gold it couldn't have sounded better. "Really?"

In response, he scooped Mikey from her lap with one hand and pulled her to her feet with the other. "Really. Go get ready and meet me downstairs in an hour."

She showered in record time and slipped into a halter dress. A break was precisely what she needed to get on terra firma again. Then things with Mikey would start clicking.

Poor baby. He probably couldn't figure out why he suddenly lived in a new place with new people. Everything familiar had been ripped away from Mikey and all she wanted to do was provide stability. Give him a sense of connection and of being cared for.

Maybe she should cancel Fort Worth.

No, she needed time away to recharge and it was the perfect opportunity to move forward with giving Shay parenting lessons.

She'd taken a seat in the sunroom when Shay strolled in and set off a new round of hot flushes.

She was tired. If she could get some decent sleep, Shay walking into a room wouldn't affect her at all. She'd never noticed when Eric came into a room. When she was absorbed in research or a case study, he'd shake her shoulder to get her attention. Eric possessed a fine list of qualities—he was unassuming, quiet and easy to ignore when she needed to concentrate. Everything she wanted in a man, and not a frustrating, stubborn, vibrating-with-masculinity boy wonder.

Eric and Shay were barely from the same planet and comparing them had grown into an unproductive habit. The two men she'd once cared for were nothing alike. Intentionally.

"Ready?" he asked.

She nodded and it wasn't until they arrived at Shay's airport that she thought to ask a really, really late question. "How are we getting there?"

"Helicopter. It's only a couple hours there and back, depending on the wind."

And how many hours if the pilot didn't fly like a kamikaze bat out of hell? She bit her lip. He understood the importance of Mikey's welfare and wouldn't take unnecessary risks. Not anymore.

"Can't we fly in a plane?"

"Sure, but then I have to land at a municipal airport. I can put the bird down on the roof of GGS. Saves me a lot of time and trouble. I fly planes to relax, not for work."

Relax. Really?

The helicopter sat on the runway like a giant black-and-glass insect. Its blades threw huge shadows on the ground and she swallowed. People rode in helicopters all the time. Nothing to worry about. Helicopter crashes were rare. Except in combat, but those crashes were due to being shot down. Weren't they?

This one had doors. Thankfully. She sat in the passenger seat and shut her eyes as Shay did whatever pilot checks were necessary and talked to people through the radio in his headset. His voice settled her and she peeked out from under her lashes.

She could do this. He'd had a license to fly everything under the sun since before she'd met him ten years ago. Surely he was even more practiced now.

Thwack, thwack, thwack.

The blades spun and, as if by magic, the helicopter lifted into the air, guided expertly by the magician at the controls. Shay's fingers wrapped firmly around the lever between their seats and he performed innumerable other sleight-of-hand tricks in rapid succession. The ground rushed away and the sky opened in a burst of blue.

The ground was *so far* below the flimsy metal cage between her and a free fall. The ground was completely unreachable, except through Shay's wizardry.

Her stomach did the tango and her eyes slammed shut again. Had he said *two* hours?

Miraculously, they did not crash, her eyelids eventually opened and about a kajillion white-knuckle deep breaths later, Shay touched down with a light bounce on a giant X. He helped her down from the high seat and she sucked oxygen into her lungs in a cleansing sigh as her shoes flattened against the roof of GGS.

"Not so bad, right?" Shay's hand settled into the small of her back and she leaned into the support gratefully. Illogically so, since it was his fault she needed steadying.

"Not so bad in comparison to jumping out of it with a parachute, perhaps."

Shay laughed and no, it wasn't so bad. Downtown Fort Worth spread out beyond the lip of the roof, twinkling in the morning light, and a much-needed break was in her future. She'd try to forget about the looming second helicopter ride, sure to come right after lunch.

Juliana took her time exploring the shops in Sundance Square and tried to enjoy a couple of hours without responsibilities, but Mikey wasn't far from her thoughts. She sent a cowboy hat to her dad and a pair of lovely turquoise earrings to her assistant. Her mom hated everything so Juliana had given up buying her gifts a long time ago.

A push-button toy decorated with music notes caught her eye. She pressed one of the squares and smiled as Mozart floated from the hidden speaker. Mozart had been her favorite to play and she suddenly missed feeling the music flow through her. Shay's casual mention of the violin the other night had shaken loose forgotten memories and since then, with greater and greater frequency, she recalled how much she'd loved to play.

She purchased the toy. Her throat tightened with a twinge of sadness because it would probably be the only gift she'd ever give Mikey. If she did her job, Mikey would have an amazing parent in Shay. She had no business dissolving into melancholy over the end of her consulting job.

Near noon, she walked the four or five blocks to the steak house Shay had suggested for lunch. Before the words "reservation for Michael Shaylen" completely left her mouth, the maître d' whisked her to a cozy corner table with multiple apologies for the apparent crime of being forced to seat her alone. Poor man. She'd adjusted to Shay-Standard-Time long ago.

He blew in fifteen minutes later and she experienced yet another difficult-to-reconcile change. Oh, he was still Shay in his T-shirt sporting a graphic of the Milky Way galaxy and an arrow pointing to the center, with the words You Are Here printed above it.

But he was also Michael Shaylen, the billionaire entrepreneur.

Every waiter in the place snapped to attention. Other diners whispered behind their hands or stared at him as he sauntered across the room. He'd always turned heads but this was different, as if the balance of his bank account also bestowed a particular mystique.

To her, he was Shay and always would be. At least his fortune would ensure Mikey would never have to make new friends in a town where his parents' creditors hadn't located them yet. Mikey would have the stability so critical for his well-being, and by the time Juliana finished with Shay's lessons, Mikey would have a good father, too.

Shay followed the maître d', oblivious to everything in the room except Juliana.

The flush hit higher in her chest this time. He could be doing a lot of other things with his day but he wasn't. His intense gaze could be fixated on a million issues surely competing for his attention. But it wasn't.

His gaze was on her.

How had a quiet, violin-playing psychology major caught the attention of such a man? He deserved someone who could match him, crazy step for crazy step.

Every nerve in her body ruffled. She didn't want to be the center of so much concentration, so much focus, so much Shay. Already she could feel it sucking at her, drawing her into the whirlpool. Speeding up her pulse, causing the ground to rush away.

Like in college, but worse—it was somehow more powerful now.

Shay slid into the opposite seat and smiled. "Did you have a good day?"

Breath rushed out of her lungs.

He could only affect her if she let him. They weren't involved, weren't going to be. Mikey and the notes for her book were the only reasons she was here.

"Yes, very good. Thank you for suggesting it. I enjoyed the time away but I'm ready to get back to work. We need to talk about the next steps."

A tiny corner of her heart wondered what Shay might be like going forward. Surely he'd no longer court danger now that he had a son. Surely he'd pay close attention if she told him how important it was to slow down.

Shay ordered quickly and dismissed the nervous waiter. "Why don't we talk about that later? We'll have lunch, just the two of us, and worry about real life in a little while."

Of course. That's what he'd always done. Worried about real life some other time.

Once, she'd appreciated the quality, had been attracted to it. *Very* attracted, because she tended to become mired in real life, constantly worried about studying enough, practicing violin enough, saving enough money or worrying about some other fill-in-the-blank disastrous circumstance she hadn't prepared for. Shay distracted her, pulled her away from her lists and agendas, drew her into spontaneity and the corporeal as only he could.

In turn, he'd learn to be more cautious from her. They'd balance each other—or that's what she'd thought would happen. Gradually, it became clear she did all the giving and he did all the taking, with zero compromise. Implausibly, he got wilder and more uninhibited the longer they were together.

So she'd ended it, convinced he needed someone braver, stronger in spirit, while she required a relationship conducted on the ground. And she'd do well to remember that in the present.

"I'd rather talk now. We have limited time and I won't extend our consultation period. My clients need me."

His eyes scrunched. He was clearly not happy. "Okay. What do you want to talk about?"

She allowed a small victory smile. Good to know she could hold her ground with him. "Let's discuss your criteria for a nanny. Until that's settled, we can't really dive into fatherhood basics as deeply as I'd prefer."

"I don't want to hire a nanny right now."

"Why not? We can't keep up trading off nighttime baby duty like we have been and still have energy left over for your crash course. I'm confident you can find a nanny with excellent references. In fact, why not hire Donna's?"

Donna's nanny would know how to handle Mikey's stomach problems and could take over middle-of-the-night feedings. Those were the most difficult times. Not because of the lack of sleep, but because Juliana couldn't help dreaming about a world where the baby in her arms belonged to her.

"References aren't the issue. Yeah, Mikey's difficult, but I don't mind a challenge. Here's the thing." He exhaled noisily. "Grant and Donna were like superparents, balancing the demands of a billion-dollar company with Mikey."

"How so?"

Shay latched onto the subject with animation. "You should have seen how much they loved Mikey. Donna took him everywhere, board meetings, lunch, always inside a sling-type deal she wore across her shoulders. Of course, he wasn't as fussy then. Sometimes Grant would take him. They tried to spend as much time with him as they could and still get the job done."

If Mikey hadn't always had stomach problems, Donna must have been breastfeeding and kept Mikey with her at work when she could to maintain his eating schedule. Juliana still couldn't picture Donna as a nurturer, but then she hadn't laid eyes on Mikey's mother in eight years. A lot could have happened in that length of time. Regardless, love wasn't the only component to being a good mother.

Shay went on. "For whatever reason, they trusted me to be the same kind of parent. I have to live up to their belief in me, have to do everything the way I know they'd want. Eventually, I'll hire a nanny, but for now, I'd like to spend more time with Mikey before throwing another person in front of him."

"I can respect that." She had to admit he'd taken the responsibility foisted upon him and handled it better than most people would have. Better than she'd expected of him. "I think they chose well when they gave Mikey to you."

Shay lit up, eyes glowing, and she didn't even attempt to squelch the flush. Didn't do any good anyway.

Juliana would bring up the nanny requirements again in a week or so. She needed to separate her emotions from the job and a nanny was critical to doing so.

They ate lunch and talked about everything but Mikey, as Shay had originally suggested. She might have protested except her brain was occupied with watching his mouth move.

Perpetual stubble lined his jaw and she couldn't stop thinking about how it felt when he used to drag that stubble across her skin. Her thighs clamped together involuntarily as her abdomen gave a long, liquid pull—the kind she hadn't experienced in a long eight years but which happened with alarming frequency now.

Stop it. Right now, she instructed her lower half.

Shay hadn't tried to make another move since the first day. Oh, she could still see the shamelessly apparent attraction in his eyes, but he'd respected her insistence that they should be friends. They weren't getting involved.

She nursed her resolve until they stepped back onto the roof of GGS with the bug-eyed helicopter staring at her, his metal mouth curled in a sneer.

"You okay?" Shay asked, and suddenly, her hand was in his.

"Fine," she lied. She could never be fine while he was touching her and looking at her with a combination of gentle concern and evident awareness.

"You trust me, right?"

"Of course." *Mostly.* "Only it's too open and too fast and I have no control."

Descriptive of both the helicopter and Shay.

"Then close your eyes." He helped her along by placing his fingertips on her eyelids and shutting them with the lightest pressure. He pulled her against his strong body—and oh, yes, it was still wall-to-wall solid muscle—and wrapped an arm around her. "Don't think about all that. I've got you. I won't let you go. Unless you want me to."

Did she want him to let go? A light breeze lifted her hair, but then it became his fingers, sliding along her neck, threading through the strands. His breath spread across her face and she registered the heat of his lips a moment before they touched hers.

Her knees loosened and she clutched at his shoulders. To keep her balance, not in surrender, but he mistook it as such.

In two-point-Shay seconds, he hefted her deeper into his arms and kissed her thoroughly, properly. Her blood woke up, frozen after so long without the perfect wizardry of Shay's hard mouth and hard body. Heat surged, enlivening everything inside, filling her to bursting. His mouth sang against hers and she spun in a whirl of dense, dark sensation, about a millisecond from going under.

Gasping, she twisted away, stumbling. Physically and mentally. "I can't."

And that was all she could squeeze out around the ice lodged in her throat and the skittery pulse stabbing in her chest.

Had she unknowingly sent him the wrong signal at lunch? She couldn't have.

She wouldn't be sucked into him, losing all sense of up or down, all sense of her goals, only to be left behind yet again. Only to fall short and constantly be aware that she could never be enough for him.

No, she didn't want Shay's unique brand of screaming-hot, brain-melting sex, not anymore. Safe, unassuming men— that's what she preferred.

Shay's kind of chaos led to heartbreak.

He cocked his head, watching her with those Shay eyes. "I won't apologize. You can't deny that was good."

"So is chocolate but it makes you fat and it's poisonous to dogs."

"I don't think I'll ask which one of us is the dog in this scenario." All traces of sensuality melted from his expression and she tried to tell herself she didn't miss it. "If you're okay to fly, we'll leave in a few minutes. I'm waiting on a couple of people I'm taking back with us."

"You're taking additional passengers? Who?"

"Candidates interested in joining GGS. I interviewed a few this morning and the two I like are coming to check out the space tourist facilities near the house."

That's what he'd been doing in Fort Worth? "I'm surprised you're still going forward with the spaceship thing, given that's how Mikey's parents died. Maybe you can read some nice Heinlein or Asimov like normal space geeks instead?"

He didn't smile. "Those who can, do. Those who can't, live vicariously through books."

The barb buried itself in the dead center of her chest and spread with hot pinpricks, a thousand times more piercing because of the yet-to-fade reaction from his mouth on hers.

He was right. She couldn't be a parent so she'd write a book. Couldn't find the answers to help Mikey *because* she'd only read books.

Without missing a beat, he finished the evisceration. "The prototype that exploded was Donna's design, but the mission statement is mine. All those stars are millions of miles away, but why would we be able to see their light unless it's to spur us to reach for them?"

"Shay." Her voice broke. "The stars are so far away to remind us Earth is where we belong."

They'd had this same argument a hundred times. How did it still have such a serrated edge? Because she'd fooled herself into thinking he'd gladly stay safe for Mikey's sake but in reality, nothing could keep him on the ground.

Four

After a thorough tour, Shay settled his top two candidates in the guest quarters and instructed the staff to see to their welfare until tomorrow morning, when Shay would fly them back to Fort Worth. He rarely had guests but the staff would handle it, as they did everything else.

It was one of the perks of money and he'd easily adapted to having every whim granted. His accountant insisted Shay overpaid for the privilege, but one guy couldn't spend the fortune he'd amassed in four lifetimes.

Shay vaulted up the back steps of the main house and made a mental note to follow up with his architect. The wakeboard lake looked mighty big and inviting and he'd like it walled off A.S.A.P.

Juliana and Mikey were in the nursery, spread out on a big quilt with a bunch of bright picture books. Mikey was sitting up with a rattle clutched in a chubby fist and when Juliana turned the page, he banged the picture with the business end of the rattle.

Juliana laughed and Shay felt an answering tug at his mouth. "What are you reading?"

She glanced up, her smile faltering. "*Goodnight Moon*. He seems to like it."

That aborted kiss still burned between them. He hadn't broken through her Dr. Cane facade quite as quickly as he'd told himself he would. Neither had she gotten over the knee-jerk desire to put her thumb on him. She still refused to see the stuff she wanted him to quit comprised a vital part of him.

But she was definitely rattled.

"You should read *Where the Wild Things Are*. That was my favorite."

Her eyebrows came together. "That's a really dark story with scary pictures. He's too young."

"Nah. It's about a boy having an adventure."

Once, he'd been determined to lift her out of that practical place. Never had he met someone so serious and he'd made a heroic effort to unwind her. When it worked—wow. But gradually, all the fun and first-love goofiness gave way to fights about whether he should be allowed to go rock climbing or sky diving or or or. Honestly, he'd have been happy to find something they could both do.

Water under the bridge. Now his life was about what felt good and what didn't. He'd work on rattling her some more because that kiss had been *hot*. She wanted him, no matter what lies she told herself.

Juliana scrunched up her face comically at Mikey instead of mounting a psychological offensive against Shay's choice of literature or continuing her argument about why the stars were so maddeningly far away.

"Did your interviews go well?" she asked with apparent genuine interest.

"Pretty well. One kid is really sharp and we got along, even though he actually finished his sentence at MIT. I won't hold it against him. He'll get passed along to some high-up suits for a second interview."

Executives and Shay comprised the core of GGS now. Together, they'd navigate the problems with the space tourist initiative and keep the company on a profitable path. Without Grant and Donna.

"Was it hard? To do the interviews?"

He'd have laid odds on her pulling back into herself after breaking off the kiss, but he was grateful she hadn't. "Yeah. It was weird to ask strangers questions about stuff I've only talked to Grant and Donna about. But the vacancies in GGS won't fill themselves."

The catch in his voice softened her expression and her compassion steadied him. He'd forgotten how perceptive she was, but not how much he liked talking to her. He'd never had the urge to talk to any of the handful of girlfriends he'd had since college. Words had been exchanged, sure, but not anything of importance. Rocket science and uncertainty weren't the stuff of casual conversation.

Mikey threw the rattle in Juliana's lap and she handed it back to him, then focused her attention on Shay. "I'm sorry. I hope it gets easier for you soon."

That's why he liked talking to her. She listened, pointedly, somehow weaving into their conversation a sense that he was the most important person in her world. "Thanks. Me, too."

Maybe he'd misread her reluctance on the roof of GGS and she'd backed off not because she wanted him to be some other guy who moved at the speed of a turtle, but because she still had a notion they should keep it professional. Which was ridiculous. It took two to create a vibe and she'd totally kissed him back.

This consulting gig was the perfect situation to feed that fire. She could teach him to be a parent, heat up his bed at night and then go back to New Mexico without getting bogged down in their philosophical differences.

If he could get her to stop with all the analysis and concentrate on how good they were together. How good they could make each other feel. He'd convince her of it.

Sex—good. Broken heart—bad.

Mikey kicked his leg, pulling a smile from Juliana. She glanced at Shay. "Maria said Mikey's responding well to the new formula. Probably a fluke. We'll get our fussy baby back tonight, I'm sure. I'm starting to suspect he's teething."

"Fan-freaking-tastic. I was thinking we needed to add another issue on top of the existing ones." Poor guy. So tiny to have so many things going on with his body.

She deposited a toy in front of Mikey and pushed a button. Classical music sailed out of it, to the baby's delight. And Shay's—there was something about all that angst and ecstasy squeezed down into the notes that spoke to a place deep inside.

"Comes with the territory," she said. "As soon as they grow out of one stage, they hit another one. Fortunately, it slows as they get older. There are a lot of stages from birth to two."

The thought of Mikey growing older scared the pants off him. One day, the baby would be able to talk and argue and wreck the car.

Shay shuddered. "That's the stuff I need to learn. You make it seem so easy, with all that knowledge right there in your brain for easy reference."

Frowning, she swept a lock of hair behind her ear. "Memorizing a textbook is easy. Being a parent isn't. Sit down and I'll go over a few of the stages. Stop me if you have questions."

As she lectured, he contented himself with watching her face. It glowed. This baby stuff really got her going and it seemed wrong she'd been thus far unsuccessful having one of her own. No matter what happened with Mikey, she never got frazzled or appeared uncertain. She had *mom* written all over her.

Mikey gurgled over his rattle in rare happiness. Shay had

a promising candidate to fill one of the big gaping holes in GGS and he was at peace. Not a bad way to fly.

His phone jangled and startled Mikey, who fell over with a wail. Juliana scooped him up, murmuring. Shay answered his cell automatically and cursed. He'd been enjoying the moment. Anxious to end the call, Shay listened with half an ear to his lawyer, Dean Abbott, babble until the word *custody* captured his full attention. He leaped to his feet, sending the rocker crashing into the wall behind it.

"Repeat that," Shay commanded, pulse pounding in both temples, and listened as Dean tore his world in two.

Dazed, he pocketed the phone and rubbed his eyes.

"What's wrong?" Juliana asked.

"Grant's parents are petitioning for custody of Mikey. They don't agree with you. They don't think a single father who makes exploding spaceships is a good choice."

They were wrong.

Grant had named Shay—not his parents—in the will for a reason and none of them could go back and ask why. All Shay could do was live up to Grant's faith in him. Mikey was Grant's son, the only piece Shay had left of his friend, the brother of his soul.

He'd never abandon Mikey.

"Oh, Shay." Juliana stood quickly and crossed to him, Mikey firmly squished against her side.

Somehow she ended up in Shay's arms in a group hug. The light fragrance of Juliana mingled with Mikey's wet-cereal and baby-lotion smell.

"They can't have him. Mikey is mine," he said.

Shay clung to them both, helpless to come up with a reason to let either of them go.

Juliana slept fitfully that night. It wasn't even her turn with Mikey until 4:00 a.m. but her lids refused to stay closed. If she wasn't reliving The Kiss or unsuccessfully trying to banish it from her mind, she was obsessing over the haunted look in Shay's eyes after he'd learned Grant's parents were petitioning for custody.

She watched the bright fish explore the coral in the tank across from her bed and ached for Shay. He tried so hard to put Mikey first, rarely letting his grief or uncertainty hinder him, but both were there, flitting under the surface.

Unfortunately, there was a chance the Greenes wouldn't lose. She'd testified at custody hearings in the past on behalf of a client's parents. Black-and-white facts were all the court could use to render its best judgment. On paper, Shay looked like a bad bet.

In reality…well, that was more complicated. He loved Mikey. She wished she could be sure that was enough but love didn't automatically equate to good parenting. Just like love didn't mean two people belonged together.

At four, she rose from bed and groggily set off for the nursery. Mikey cried and cried, no matter what she did. Would a real mother do something differently? If Juliana had carried Mikey in her womb for nine months, would helping him still be this difficult? If his adoptive father wasn't such a distraction, would her knowledge come more easily?

"Try something else," Shay suggested from the doorway.

She glanced up. He was leaning on the door frame, hip casually holding up the wall, and plain flannel pants slung sinfully low. Or maybe it was the lack of a shirt that screamed sin, because holy mother of God—he was still built like a centerfold model.

"I've tried everything," she shot back and averted her eyes before they started smoking. "You see where it got me. Go back to bed. It's my turn. You should be sleeping."

The custody suit must be weighing on him, like it had with her.

"I've been trying to sleep. A connecting room means you

can hear through the walls. I don't know why I bothered to get a monitor. Did you give him the medicine?"

"No." She scooted back an inch but the rocker curved her back uncomfortably. Everything was uncomfortable in the middle of the night. Especially when Shay was shirtless. "I want to see how the new formula works instead."

Shay frowned and crossed his arms, a posture he assumed when forced to be still. The motion sent a ripple down his hard-to-miss pectoral muscles. "The doctor said to give the medicine a few days. He only cried for thirty minutes at the last feeding."

"But he still cried." She boosted Mikey higher on her shoulder. "That's not the definition of *working*."

"Ju, you have to give him the medicine. Why did I call the doctor if you're not going to do what he said?"

The honeymoon—that brief period where she knew what she was doing and Shay listened to her—was over. "Only a pediatrician can make an accurate diagnosis and I wanted to be sure about what I'm dealing with. I tried the medicine and now I'm trying something else."

"He's my kid."

The quiet declaration of Shay's authority twisted her stomach. She knew whose baby she held and he wasn't hers. Shay couldn't possibly know she sometimes wished otherwise. Could he?

"The medicine the doctor gave you is new. One day, the news will report it causes prostate cancer. Or premature aging. Or something else they haven't discovered yet."

"Okay." He threw up his hands. "Back off, Mama-saurus. Going at each other isn't helping."

"It makes me feel better." She didn't go as far as sticking her tongue out but she wanted to.

Mama-saurus. It was the kind of nickname a loving husband gave the mother of his children, not the kind a client gave to a consultant hired to teach a man about parenting but who couldn't seem to handle one small baby. "Go sleep in another room if Mikey's too loud."

And put a shirt on.

"Yeah, I'm going," Shay grumbled and vanished from the doorway.

With all the distractions gone, she rocked and soothed the fussy baby, clasping him tightly to her as he bawled. He finally fell asleep and stayed asleep, but she didn't move from the rocker. With his little face relaxed and his chest gently rising and falling, it was the closest thing to heaven on earth she'd ever experienced. Babies were a miracle mere mortals could hold in their own two hands.

Her thoughts drifted along with the motion of the chair and of course the baby's father popped right into her head.

While Shay wouldn't have been *her* first choice for Mikey's guardian, he had been Grant's and Donna's. Likely they'd known a side of him rarely on display to the public. From what Shay had told her, Grant's parents were cold and judgmental, particularly Mr. Greene, and Grant had rarely agreed with his father on anything. Additionally, the baby's grandparents must be aging. How did they expect to keep up with an active toddler? Who would take over if one or both of them became infirm—or died?

No doubt they had the baby's welfare at heart, but so did Shay. She was convinced of it. Otherwise they wouldn't butt heads over Mikey's care. If Shay planned to keep custody, he needed help. Documenting the steps he'd taken to learn how to be a father wouldn't be enough.

But she had an idea of what might be enough.

Once it had been daylight for a good hour, she hoisted Mikey into the crook of her arm and went in search of Shay. She found him in the straight-out-of-*Architectural-Digest* dining room, shoveling half a pig and a whole chicken coop's worth of eggs into his mouth. Dressed, thank goodness.

"Eating the breakfast of champions, I see," she said.

Shay flashed a melty, goofy smile at the baby. Her ridiculous hot flushes weren't at all discerning. He wasn't even smiling at her.

"What's wrong with bacon and eggs? Animals exist for people to eat."

"In moderation," she said, doubtful he knew the definition of the word. "Bacon contains enough sodium to stop the heart of an elephant, and eggs are full of cholesterol."

His eyebrows rose and he forked a heaping pile of eggs into his mouth in an exaggerated "neener-neener." He swallowed and said, "Nothing a good, sweaty workout won't cure. Want to help me work it off?"

A hazardous, predatory glint flashed in his eyes—one that said he wasn't talking about lifting weights. The flush was more of a hammer to the abdomen this time. It was getting really hard to chalk up her response to fatigue.

She *was* tired. But she also had to admit sheer will alone couldn't combat her very feminine reaction to this shamelessly stimulating man. When he'd kissed her, he'd woken up her sex drive and no amount of coaxing, bargaining or stern admonishment could put it back to sleep.

She ignored the swirl inside her. Mind over matter. She had a job to do and her professionalism was suffering.

"Shay, we have to talk about the custody petition. I'm happy to testify on your behalf, but it's not enough. You have a difficult fight ahead, which you might lose if you don't make some changes."

"I'm not going to lose." He scowled at his plate and shoved it away. "Grant's parents are devastated and not thinking straight. They blame me for the explosion and this is just a ploy to cause me grief. What judge will take away a baby from someone with my financial ability to care for Mikey? Don't forget the will, either. Both his parents signed it."

"A judge will look at the bigger picture. Being able to afford the best for Mikey is not the most relevant factor, and neither is a will. You're not a blood relative, and you're not married, nor are you dating anyone seriously."

An image of a swimsuit model draped across his soft, fluffy mattress sprang to mind. She swallowed the urge to remind him how important maternal instincts were in his choice of companions. There was nothing inherently wrong with swimsuit models and Shay could date whomever he wanted. The tightness in her throat didn't ease.

"So? Single parents raise kids all the time."

"They do, but when there's a question of custody, a judge will determine the best possible environment for Mikey. A single parent with dangerous hobbies and business ventures that have already proven fatal might raise some eyebrows. Plus, the Greenes are the baby's biological grandparents."

"I don't care. They can't have Mikey."

She sank into the chair next to him, eye to eye, and bounced Mikey. "Then let's create an environment the judge will be reluctant to remove him from."

"How, Juliana?" he barked and scrubbed at his stubble. "Are you saying I have to get married to win?"

"Not at all. Being single is only one mark against you. There are other things we can do. We're going to give you a makeover."

He eyed her. "Like that time you painted my fingernails?"

The memory swam into focus. The power had failed during a doozy of a Texas thunderstorm and instead of braving the soaking rain, they'd plowed through a bottle of wine by candlelight and played card games. One silly bet led to another and when Juliana's king beat Shay's queen, he had to let her paint his fingernails. He'd moaned bitterly about it but in the end, honored his word. Shay would never agree to something and then back out.

It had been fun, an infrequent slice of time when the real world couldn't penetrate their bubble.

She'd forgotten about that night. Forgotten what it felt like to have uncensored fun without constantly worrying about *something.* Being around Shay again tempted her—often— to let go of her rigid constraints. But history had showed the result of that mistake and to avoid repeating it, she'd have to hold her professionalism close at all costs.

"Not a fashion-and-hair makeover," she corrected, her Dr. Cane voice sailing out of her mouth. "A lifestyle makeover. If you want to keep Mikey, eliminate as many objectionable issues as possible. The court will appoint a guardian *ad litem,* who will visit Mikey's home and ask a lot of questions. You need to make major, visible changes before then. Then the Greenes' petition will have no traction."

"My life is exactly the way I want it," he said, his tone full of all-too-familiar stubbornness. "Anyone who doesn't like it can get their own life."

"That's exactly what Grant's parents are trying to do. Get their own life, with Mikey. If you want to take your chances, be my guest. Your money can't buy another one of Grant's children."

Frustrated, edgy and aware half of her agitation had to do with lingering tension over The Kiss and shirtless middle- of-the-night-conversations, she raised Mikey to her hip and stood to leave.

Shay stopped her with a firm grip on her elbow. "Wait. I'm sorry. I know you're trying to help. I'm listening."

She sank back into the ebony dining chair. Shay hadn't re- moved his fingers and the contact flickered across her skin. But she refused to glance at his hand. "Brutal truth, Shay. You have to slow down and stay out of trouble. No more he- licopters as your primary means of transportation. No more superhero cars. No extreme sports. No more—"

"That's a lot of restrictions." His fingers finally dropped away to restlessly drum the table. "What are you suggesting, that I become someone else?"

"Yes. A father. Look it up in the dictionary. It's defined

by *sacrifice*. This is what you hired me for, to help you learn what it takes to be a parent Grant and Donna would be proud of." She met his gaze and held it. "The Greenes' lawyer could throw a rock and hit someone who can testify how many broken bones you've had in the last few years. You boldly paraded candidates intended to replace the Greenes' son through GGS, signifying your intent to move forward with the spaceship prototype. The prototype that killed Mikey's parents. Are you starting to get my drift?"

This custody suit, while difficult and heart-wrenching, proved her point about Shay's obsession with danger. It might be the only thing to get through his thick skull since not even becoming a father had.

His lips pursed. "You think I should shut down the space tourist division. Scrap three years of work to prove to a judge I'm not going to go out the same way as Grant and Donna."

Good, he wasn't playing dumb. The spaceship madness had to go, no doubt, but she'd learned eight years ago that he wouldn't change just because she asked him to. The idea had to be his. "As an act of good faith. It will show beyond a shadow of a doubt that Mikey is your first priority. That's what the judge will want to see. Unless you're willing to let someone else test the capsule."

He shook his head. Vehemently. "No one else goes up in my spaceship."

"Well, then—"

"Maybe, instead, my lawyer can document my mission statement. To create safe, affordable space travel for average citizens. I'm not planning to blow up more million-dollar machinery, especially not with me or anyone else inside it. I know exactly what to do differently with the fuel line. Space is the final frontier and I'm blazing the trail." He broke off and stared at the wall behind Juliana's head. "That won't help my case, will it?"

Well, well. Progress. More than she'd ever made in college, when she'd failed miserably at explaining how hard it would be to lose him when she loved him so much. How scary it was to let him fly without knowing if he'd come back. It would be even harder on Mikey to lose another father, especially the only one he'd remember.

"I'm sorry." As long as she'd known Shay, he'd reached for the stars. She'd left him in part so he could chase his dreams. It killed her to have to be the voice of reason. "I know what I'm saying isn't easy to hear. But it's for the best."

"The best for whom? Mikey or you?"

"This isn't about me and you. I'm advocating this course of action for Mikey's benefit. And because I believe in you. We have to ensure everyone can see your commitment to Mikey in tangible, quantifiable ways. Think about it, okay?"

The carved-in-granite lines of his face didn't waver. "I'll think about it. And talk to my lawyer."

The weight on her chest should have lifted.

It didn't.

Because she'd lied.

If he did what she proposed, it didn't only benefit Mikey. Her heart thrilled at the idea of a grounded Shay. A safe Shay. This makeover had an excellent chance of swaying the judge in Shay's favor. But it would also turn Shay into the man she'd once been convinced he'd never be. After a childhood lived in fear and constantly being shuttled from new home to new home, she wanted the steadiness of someone who would be there for her through all the trials of life, who would never leave her, emotionally or physically.

The opposite of the upheaval Shay had represented in college.

But if he took her advice, he could become the kind of man she could envision being with forever.

If he took her advice, maybe they could turn The Kiss into something more.

Five

Shay dusted his hands with white chalk and reached up for the initial crevice in the fifty-foot rock wall on the south side of his property.

Climb. Don't think. *Climb.*

This was his fourth trip up the sheer face. Sweat stung his eyes but he ignored it. If he scaled the wall about a hundred more times, maybe then he'd calm down enough to be civilized in mixed company.

His body gave out well before hitting the hundredth climb. Chest heaving, he dropped onto the manicured grass and stared at the cloudless blue sky. Nope. Still mad as hell and the sharp sting along his shin meant he'd left skin on the wall.

Grant's parents hadn't brought up the custody petition to cause problems, despite what he'd told Juliana. They wanted Mikey because he was their grandson. Rationally, he knew that, like he knew the pain and grief they must feel. He shared both, coupled with an unconditional intention to justify Grant's faith in his ability to raise Mikey.

Neither should he be furious with Juliana for bringing up logical points about his unorthodox life, points which, in retrospect, did have a chance of being a problem with the court.

But he *was* furious.

While Juliana's suggestions pricked at festering wounds, she'd had her sights set on this ridiculous custody battle, not him. Not *them*.

He had to get a grip and stop blaming Juliana for displaying the levelheadedness he valued in her.

If he couldn't be mad at the Greenes and he couldn't be mad at Juliana, he could only be mad at himself for being mad about an impossible situation and no amount of rock climbing, Cessna flying or Hayabusa riding would cure that. Though he'd tried.

Disgusted, he sprinted at full speed up the two hundred yards to the back steps of the house, and stormed into his bedroom to drown his horrible mood in a scalding shower. Too late, he remembered the shredded skin below his knee and swore as the hot water lit up the wound and lathered up as quickly as possible.

Once he dried off, he doctored the scrape, which wasn't nearly as bad as the one from Agulha do Diabo—which had never healed quite right thanks to subpar tropical medical care—but wasn't as shallow as the nick he'd gotten from El Capitan in Yosemite.

He yanked on a T-shirt and cargo shorts because he refused to hide the scrape with jeans. He was Shay and that wasn't changing anytime soon, whether anyone else appreciated it or not.

Juliana was coming up the twisty staircase as he descended. Her eye gravitated to the large white bandage on his leg, but she didn't comment. His mood shifted a molecule toward the pleasant side.

"Got a few minutes?" she asked.

She looked cool and sophisticated in a crisp halter-top

sundress, hair caught back in a clippy thing. The kind that opened easily if you squeezed the butterfly wings.

His fingers tingled. He'd like nothing better than to release her hair, letting it fall free into his palm. With his muscles warmed and still buzzing from the ruthless workout, it wouldn't take much to shoot his heart rate back up into the zone and he was primed for it.

"Depends." He cocked his head and let his gaze slide down her body suggestively. Her halter top was the string-tie variety, looped into a tempting bow at her neck. It wasn't double-knotted and could easily be pulled apart with teeth. "What do you have in mind?"

"A nanny," she responded decisively and rested a slim hand on the banister as she peered up at him. "I know you're still thinking about what we discussed this morning and I'm not trying to pressure you, but a good nanny will only help your case, especially given the lack of a second parent in the home."

Shay crossed his arms before yanking out that clip became a reality instead of a fantasy, and leaned a hip against the banister, an inch from her fingers.

"Yeah? I was gonna do the nanny thing anyway. No time like the present. Is that all you wanted?"

"Well." Her clear blue irises radiated as she jumped head-first into the subject. "We have to discuss what you're looking for. Once we have a list, then we can contact some agencies. Do you know if Donna's nanny is still unemployed? She might be the most logical place to start."

Nodding once, he slid his hip right up next to her hand. She didn't notice. Too involved in her discourse on the process of nanny hiring.

"Let's go with that. We'll hire Mikey's former nanny, whom he already knows and vice versa, and Grant's parents will have no good reason to complain about it. Problem solved."

Juliana made a cute face. "Hardly. What if she's already found another job? What if—"

He did reach out then and closed her mouth with his fingers. "Shh. We'll worry about whether the nanny is already employed later. Where's Mikey?"

She shook his fingers off. "I left him with Maria so we could *talk*."

"Lo and behold, that seems to be what we're doing."

From his vantage point, the neckline of her dress dipped just the right way to reveal the inside curve of her breast. The back of his neck heated.

"Uh-huh. You seem very interested in talking."

He shrugged and went for innocence. "Words are coming out of my mouth, aren't they?"

"It's the nonverbal I'm referring to," she said with raised eyebrows.

"Really?" He advanced a step. Only two separated them now, but she didn't retreat, like he'd expected. Now he was getting somewhere. "What's my nonverbal saying?"

"It says you're interested in throwing me over your shoulder and doing very wicked things to me upstairs."

His eyes widened involuntarily. "Wow, you're good. What is *your* nonverbal saying? 'Please hurry'?"

She laughed but it was husky and affected, maybe because she was picturing those wicked things. "More like 'please get over yourself.'"

He matched her grin. His bad mood had dissolved and he was *definitely* picturing wicked things. How stupid was he for *rock climbing* as a stress reliever when he had Juliana under his roof?

"Aw, come on. It's not saying 'maybe in a little while, after Mikey's in bed'?"

She contemplated for a second, still composed, but a hint of heat deep in her gaze encouraged him. "No, it's really not saying that."

"Really, really?" In one move, he landed on the same step with her and a whiff of female curled through his blood. He wanted her good and rattled, so he reached out to trace a finger across her perfect pink lips. "Are you sure?"

Her eyelids drifted halfway closed and she exhaled, leaning ever so slightly toward him. Drawn to him, as he was to her. "I'm…sure."

Her heat wrapped around him, gliding along his nerves.

"Huh. It feels an awful lot like your nonverbal is saying something more like 'maybe I'm considering it,'" he murmured as everything south of his waist roared to life, hungry, and wondering why the stuff north of the shoulders was still blathering. "Stop thinking so much and consider this."

He crushed her against the banister and kissed her. Fed from her. Did what he'd been dying to do for what seemed like a hundred years. He kissed her with defiance. Because he wasn't sorry to be firm against her mouth again, reveling in the slide of her flesh against his, drowning in Juliana.

Yeah, this was what he'd been after since he first saw her at the foot of the stairs, since he'd kissed her at the helipad. Now he had the right outlet to vent his frustration.

He poured all that emotion into kissing her.

It was good. So enlivening, engulfing. A whole-body experience. Exactly the way he liked it. The way she melted against him demonstrated very nicely how much she liked it, too.

Maybe her head said no, but her body sang a different tune and the evidence of her desire was sweet satisfaction.

She wanted him. Just like this.

The clip came apart in his hands and he dropped it to thrust his fingers through her flaxen hair. Like gossamer filament against his flesh. He groaned and deepened the kiss, taking her mouth in heavy gulps.

She gripped his shoulders with eager hands, pulling him closer. Yeah, closer was good. He released the hair and wrapped his arms around this woman who'd once owned a piece of him.

"Mr. Shay?" A male voice cut through his lust haze, echoing through the vast foyer at the foot of the stairs.

Reluctantly, Shay stepped away and Juliana's hands slid from his back. Slowly.

"Remember where we were," he murmured and ached with the effort required to keep from hauling her back. Her kiss-stung lips glistened and he could still taste her.

Antonio, the groundskeeper, appeared at the base of the stairs, wringing his grass-stained hands. "Mr. Shay, the bambino, he fell down. Maria says come quickly."

The bambino? Oh, hell, no. "Mikey's hurt?"

Juliana was already bounding down the stairs ahead of him, as she apparently could put two and two together faster than his raging hormones had allowed.

She followed Antonio, and Shay followed her, his pulse thundering. Outside, they found Maria sitting on the concrete-and-marble-inlaid patio, clutching the baby, both of them bawling.

"What happened?" Shay demanded and only Juliana's firm grip on his arm kept him from charging forward to snatch Mikey from the maid's lap.

"He's so fast. I'm so sorry, Mr. Shay." Between sniffs, she explained how Mikey had learned to crawl and tumbled off the patio to the grass two feet below the far edge.

"What? How come you weren't watching him?" The patio needed railing and the entire backyard should have spongy playground material instead of hard dirt. "Give him to me. No, Juliana, you take him. I have to get the helicopter warmed up. I can be at the hospital in—"

"Is he bleeding?" Juliana interrupted, calmly. Maria shook her head. "Did he land on his back or his stomach?"

"I don't know...I couldn't see," she said over Mikey's wails. Juliana took Mikey and hummed, swaying back and forth and stroking his head. When he quieted, she ran a loose fist down the length of his arms and legs. She wagged her index finger in front of his eyes. "He's fine. He doesn't need to go to the hospital. There's no sign of concussion or broken bones. The fall only scared him. Babies fall down. It happens a lot."

"He shouldn't have been outside. If he's going to fall, he should fall in his room where there's carpet." Shay shifted from foot to foot, too restless to be still. He dismissed Maria and Antonio. The staff didn't need to hang around and witness his panic attack. Antonio split but Maria trundled off slowly with backward glances and more apologies, which Shay waved off.

It wasn't her fault. It was his.

"Are you sure he doesn't need a doctor to look at him?"

"What, you don't think a PhD is as good as a medical degree?" With a wry smile, Juliana handed Mikey to Shay. "Hold him and see for yourself. He's fine."

The baby hiccupped and buried his head in Shay's shoulder, wetting it with a bunch of baby drool. He did seem fine. But he was just so little. How did babies survive until their first birthday with all the dangers and new stages and clueless adults? "Maybe *you* should be the nanny."

Juliana laughed. "Overkill, Shay. Babies are more resilient than your conscience would dictate."

"I shouldn't have left him with Maria. She's in her fifties." The Greenes' court-appointed tattletale would have a field day with a disaster like this. "What was I thinking?"

"That you can't do it all. Don't let this cloud a huge milestone. Mikey learned to crawl. That's the first of many really cool baby things you get to witness as a parent."

"Yeah, cool. He learns to crawl and the first thing he does is dive off the patio. What's wrong with learning to crawl someplace without a drop-off?"

"He has to go outside sometime. Fresh air is good for him."

"Inside is good, too. We can open windows for fresh air.

Windows with bars, so he can't fall out." What else? Locks on the doors. Maybe a twenty-four-hour guard to make sure Mikey stayed safe.

"I empathize. It's hard to watch someone you care about get hurt." Her gaze bored through him.

Shay's eyes closed and he heaved out a ragged sigh. "Yeah, okay. I get it."

Silently, she waited him out. At least she hadn't come right out and called him a hypocrite. But the truth hung there, between them, alive and kicking.

For Mikey.

"I'll call Donna's nanny first thing in the morning. Then I'll move forward with the rest of the changes we talked about."

Except dismantling the space tourism division. His chest hurt to imagine archiving all the files, shutting down the facility. He'd built his house near the place where his dreams were unfolding.

But he held a different future in his arms and he'd do the right thing for Mikey.

He just couldn't do it all at once. No one would fault him for making changes slowly. Once the petition was dropped, he could pick up the space tourism plans where he'd left them. The changes Juliana talked about didn't have to be permanent. Not all of them, anyway.

He was Shay. And a father. He'd find a way to stay true to both.

In a moment of inspiration, he said, "I'm inviting Mikey's grandparents out to the house for a visit. I should have already and maybe it'll help to build a relationship with them. Show I don't plan to cut them out of his life."

"What a lovely idea." Juliana's serene smile went a long way toward loosening the tight bands around his chest. "And, Shay? About what happened on the stairs earlier…"

Instantly, his mind shifted from Mikey to the interrupted kiss. "Yeah?"

"I'm considering it. Emphasis on *considering*."

And of all that had transpired in a very short period of time, Juliana's about-face was easily the best thing that had happened that day.

It was the next day before Juliana saw Shay again.

He'd generously agreed to give her time each day to herself, so she worked at the desk in her room, typing up notes for the parenting book. The cozy alcove came stocked with every color of pen, sticky notes, paper clips, mailing supplies. Every office gadget she could have imagined. Her aging laptop seemed out of place in the midst of the high-end printer, document shredder and other things she'd likely never use.

Excess should have been Shay's middle name instead of something as teeth-numbingly bland as James.

She *was* using the intricate and sophisticated sound system, which Shay had stocked with every classical violin recording under the sun. The rich notes washed over her as she typed. Reminding her of a time when music had been just as important to her as babies. She'd stopped playing when she'd broken up with Shay.

It had been too painful to imagine that front-row-center seat vacant at her performances, and music wasn't a practical way to gain the stability she'd desperately needed. Then or now.

Shay's thoughtful inclusion of a sound system in her room made her realize how much she missed music.

A loud crash reverberated outside the window, interrupting the tranquil music for the third time in ten minutes and thankfully getting her mind off Shay. At least four different work crews tromped through the backyard alongside heavy-duty trucks in a flurry of activity, which had been going on most of the morning.

She turned up the music and focused. The outline of the book took shape under her fingers and she loved every minute of planning the chapters, organizing her thoughts. This book was her baby. She'd already contacted a colleague's agent, who'd expressed enthusiasm about the project the moment Juliana had mentioned Shay's name. The numbers the agent had thrown around would wipe out her debt.

Her entire adult life had been constructed to avoid picking up the phone to hear a creditor spewing contempt in her ear, like she'd endured her entire childhood. She could still recall the threats against her parents, threats to come take her toys and books, the humiliation.

Yes, she'd gone into debt for the chance at pregnancy, but she'd expected to have Eric's income to help. When they'd decided to divorce, it had seemed fair to accept the entire amount in the settlement since the defect was hers.

A prickle walked across her shoulders and she glanced up to see Shay leaning against the open door frame, wearing faded-in-all-the-right-places jeans, a T-shirt and a backward ball cap. His arms were crossed and a carnal smile was plastered across his stubbly jaw.

Laying eyes on that stubble set off the hot flush, which after the kiss on the stairs was more of a surge. She hadn't seen him in the flesh since yesterday, but he dominated her thoughts. Not in a client-employer way, either.

They stared at each other for a minute. An hour.

"Are you going to stand there and watch me work?" she asked when he didn't speak.

"Wasn't planning to but, then, I didn't know how sexy I would find it until I was already here."

"Typing turns you on? You should get out more." Why did her voice sound so breathy?

"Not typing. You. Especially you with bare feet and the tips of your toes peeking out from under the desk. That pink nail polish is smoking."

Her toes curled automatically and the heat in his voice zinged straight to her core. She shouldn't be still considering giving in to that heat. But she was.

Detached and professional would be best. Safest. Except ever since he'd said he would consider making changes, she'd been considering what, exactly, those wicked things he wanted to do to her might be.

He raked her body with a smoldering, appreciative once-over, which promised the things would be very wicked, indeed. It had been a long time since a man had looked at her like that.

She shook her head. It had been so long for a reason. She shouldn't be thinking about it and she never should have admitted as much to Shay.

"I know I said I was…considering, but Mikey is more than enough for both of us to deal with. Is it worth adding this—" she wagged her finger between them "—to the mix?"

"Really, Ju?" He flowed into the room and slid up next to the desk, crowding her with his vibrating masculinity. "That's the question?"

"What should I ask, then?"

He spun the chair and trapped her legs between his. Helpless to move, helpless to stop her gaze from roaming over the very powerful body inches from hers. She knew exactly what the dips and peaks under his blue T-shirt looked like. Hard. Sun-bronzed. The memory from the other night blazed across her mind's eye.

Her lungs froze as he cupped her chin.

"No questions," he murmured. "Stop trying to assign logic to something illogical. There's no explanation for why there's still this vibe between us. No explanation for why the sight of you makes me feel alive."

His fingers skated down her arm and captured her hand, drawing it upward to plaster it against his racing heart. "No explanation for why my body does this when I smell you."

"Technically, there is. It's fifty percent cognitive stimuli and—"

"Okay, fine, Dr. Cane. It's a physiological phenomenon with measurable data. Here it is." He yanked her out of the chair and into his arms, crushing her against his extreme arousal. "Get right up close and personal to that data. Feel that? I want you. Naked, with me deep inside you. Deal with it."

Oh, my. The data was impressive and her own body reacted involuntarily. She couldn't speak, couldn't think. Her insides went liquid and a shock of anticipation heated the space between her legs.

Whenever she thought it might be safe, sane and manageable with Shay, he proved her wrong. Logic evaporated when he touched her and she couldn't have that.

"Duly noted," she squawked and shoved on his rock-hard chest until he stepped back. "And you have to deal with the fact that I haven't decided if getting involved is a good idea. If it's what I want. We tried it once and it didn't work. Why should this time be any different?"

"Sometimes you do things that feel good even if they make no sense."

Her skin still tingled from his body pressing against it and, yes, it was senseless. He wanted her. If she fell into his quicksand again, then what? She'd fall for him all over again, only to be right back where she'd been in college.

"No, *you* do things that feel good and are senseless. I don't."

"You keep telling yourself that. I'll keep giving you more data. Don't lose that bottle of nail polish." He nodded to her feet. She felt his grin clear to her pink toes. "But that's not the reason I'm here. I've got some things to show you. Come with me." He held out a palm, clearly expecting her to drop everything, clasp his hand and run off with him. "I need you to give the final approval on some safety features I'm having installed. I'm sure you noticed all the guys milling around outside."

She'd been about to refuse, about to insist she was in the middle of something, but he'd see through that excuse in a second. Besides, it was a reasonable request from her employer and she couldn't resist seeing what all the activity had been about. Or the fact that he wanted her approval.

Terribly aware of her toes, she stepped into sandals, and was only a little disappointed he didn't actually try to hold her hand as he led her down the stairs to the back of the house. Her empty hand curled into a fist by her side.

West Texas heat engulfed her as she stepped outside the French door to the patio. She felt for the twenty-odd men sweating under the blistering sun. No matter how much Shay was paying them, dollar bills didn't keep anyone cool.

Shay led her down the flagstone steps to the pool, which was now surrounded by a black metal fence.

"Iron," Shay said proudly and thumped one of the square-rod spindles. "Eight feet high. Check out this gate."

He pointed to a black box welded to the iron at waist level.

"Go on, try it. Can't open it, can you?" he interjected before she'd even gotten a grip on the gate to try and swing it open. "It's biometric. That pad is a fingerprint scanner. Watch."

Shay pressed his thumb to the scanner and it turned green. The gate popped free with a buzz. He grinned that whole-face grin and she couldn't help but return the smile, though electronics and fancy gizmos weren't the reason. His obvious enthusiasm was infectious.

"Very nice." She nodded. "The gate will not only keep out Mikey but anyone else unauthorized."

"The installer will program your print as soon as you give it to him."

Her gaze followed the fence line and then shifted down the hill to the lake, about half a mile away. The workers were installing more iron fencing around the water feature. "I can't believe they've done all this in one day."

"Amazing, huh? Tomorrow, they're installing similar biometric readers inside the house on all the exterior windows and doors. I had a nightmare last night about Mikey learning to walk and letting himself out the front door. Come on, there's more."

Charmed in spite of not having a clue how to navigate his onslaught, she followed him to the huge, squat building past the pool and walked through the door into a wonderland of chrome and colors. Vehicles of every shape and size lined the black-and-white-checked floor in two neat rows.

"I didn't realize this was your garage," she said. Because most people had two-car garages, not forty-car garages. She knew next to nothing about cars but the sleek, sensual lines of the bodies were distinctly exotic and expensive.

The more time she spent with Shay, the more she realized he wasn't the same person she'd known in college. Yes, he could still kiss like the devil and still craved speed and altitude above common sense. Yes, he still did everything full-tilt, even baby-proofing, and his zeal had always been the most attractive thing about him.

But he'd also accomplished a lot. He hadn't accidentally stumbled over success. In the process of building a company from nothing, he had perhaps grown up more than she'd given him credit for. The brief glimpses of billionaire entrepreneur Michael Shaylen she'd seen thus far hadn't fully revealed the new depths that, in retrospect, had to be there.

God help her, she wanted to experience those depths. She wanted to lie down in them and roll around.

She was so torn, so not ready to deal with all the complications of getting involved with Shay again, but unsure if the complications were real or imagined.

She needed to stop thinking so much. And Shay was certainly the master of reducing her to the state of brainlessness.

Shay affectionately caressed the bumper of the nearest machine. "The garage will be something else now. I listed almost everything in here for sale and I already accepted offers on a few. The Bugatti went for a stellar profit, which I was not expecting, and the Hayabusa sold in about thirty minutes, which I was." He shrugged. "So, it's all good."

"Oh" was all she could say.

He said it so matter-of-factly, but he'd been talking about buying a Hayabusa since the first day she'd met him. At some point, he'd turned it into a reality. Now he was selling it.

Shay's hands dynamically drew out his vision in the air. "I can turn the garage into an indoor tennis court or bowling alley. Whatever Mikey's into when he gets older. I'll be a dad who listens to what my kid says he wants to do, not one who tries to get his kid to do things *he* likes."

Like his own father had.

The memory sharpened of Shay pouring out his misery late one night, his head pillowed against her stomach. Juliana had stroked his hair as he'd talked and talked, grieving about how his father didn't understand him. Mr. Shaylen had practically forced Shay to go to MIT, intending for his son to become a physics professor like him. It was to Shay's credit that he'd stayed in grad school as long as he had.

Shay wanted to be a good dad. He was making the changes to prove it. And she'd do everything in her power to help him, even making the hard calls. Even dealing with the sharp agony of helping him create a family she'd have no place in.

She filed that tidbit away for her book. Parenting was about making hard calls and living with them. Sacrifice, like she'd told him, which was difficult. Sometimes you had to give up things you'd dreamed about for years. Shay was making these sacrifices more successfully than she'd expected.

His willingness to do so certainly gave her plenty to *consider*. Like, what if it could be different this time between them? Like, what if she spent so much time analyzing, so much time searching for a safety net, she never found out?

"I talked to my pilot about being on call to fly me back and forth to GGS. In the jet, not the helicopter," he clarified and captured her hand, squeezing it. "He's very seasoned and I can get you his qualifications. I want this stuff I'm putting in place to be right. You have to tell me if it's not."

Everything—her resistance, her professionalism, her knees—melted.

Shay had grown up.

After careful consideration, she knew what she wanted—to try on a second chance with this new and improved Shay.

Six

Shay detailed a few more items before he glanced at Juliana and realized he'd lost her. She was watching him with a glazed expression, the kind his admin got when he went off on a tangent about quantum mechanics.

"So, I talked to Emily, Donna's nanny, and she's interested in the position. She's living in Fort Worth but is willing to move here. Anything else I overlooked?" he asked and she didn't answer. "Ju, still with me?"

"Which car are you keeping?"

"The Land Rover." Truth or half-truth? Well, she'd find out soon enough anyway. "And the Acura. It was a special order."

Selling the Hayabusa had almost killed him, but losing the Acura would finish the job. The only way that car was leaving this property was when they pried the key fob from his cold, dead fingers. A man had to have *something*.

"Can we sit in it?" The skirt of her frothy sundress rode up a tantalizing inch as she sauntered over to the car.

"Sure." He pulled the door open and let her slide into the

driver's seat, then took the passenger seat. "Should I start it? It's kind of boring with the engine off."

"That's okay." She pointedly examined the steering wheel and gauges. "This is a very complicated piece of machinery."

"It is. What's up, Juliana? Did you develop an interest in cars in the last five minutes or are you leading up to something?"

She shot him a sidelong glance and her expression caught him in a place he was pretty sure she hadn't intended to hit. Heat spread and his blood started pumping faster.

"I was thinking we should talk." Her fingers wrapped around the steering wheel and he couldn't stop watching her thumb rub back and forth. "We haven't done nearly enough of that."

"That's all we've done. I've been angling for a lot less talking but you're all blah, blah, blah…" He trailed off, thoroughly losing the thread of the conversation as she leaned back in the seat with a slight arch to her back. The sassy sundress she wore had straps instead of a tie-up top, and the fabric strained across her breasts.

One-handed, she gathered up her hair from her neck and smoothed it from her shoulder. The distinctive scent of Juliana—flowery and fresh—wafted in his direction and his lower half went rigid. Other women didn't smell like that.

He cleared his throat. "What did you want to talk about?"

Her head turned, cheek sliding against the soft leather of the driver's seat. She met his gaze and licked her lips. "Tell me something about your life, something the media wouldn't have reported, that's happened since college."

"Like what, I secretly wear women's underwear?"

She rolled her eyes and the garage lights spun through them like a kaleidoscope. "Why do you crack jokes when I'm trying to be serious?"

Because he couldn't read her and when unsure, jokes came out of his mouth automatically. Equations and the way parts fit together, he got. Juliana, he wanted to solve in exactly the same way but ever since his first conversation with Dr. Cane he'd been treading on unfamiliar ground. "You're always serious. My goal in life is to get you to lighten up. What should I tell you, then?"

"Something true. I want to know who you are now." Her hand came to rest on his forearm, and that kaleidoscope in her irises drew him in. "Besides a man trying to become a father."

Mesmerized, he watched her eyes and blurted out, "I started a foundation funded out of my personal accounts, but only one person on the board knows that."

"That's wonderful. What does the foundation do?"

"Gives kids investment capital to start their own businesses. Like the one that staked me and Grant." He shrugged, his skin tingling with vulnerability, like he'd stripped in front of a bunch of strangers. "It's my way of giving back, plus a couple of the companies have developed some great technology. What about you? Give me a highlight from the last eight years."

"Oh, my life has been so much less interesting than yours."

She skirted around the subject expertly by leaning into the console between their seats, her breath uneven and sexy. A heated expression on her face had him doing a double take.

"So, are you—"

She stuck her lips on his.

Shay was so surprised, he froze. She drew back with a funny sound. "Ah, I…"

With a growl, he followed her and did it right.

His mouth covered hers, molded to hers, explored hers and she moaned. Her tongue met his in the middle, and the sensuous slide of that rough texture set his blood on fire. Juliana was kissing him and it was *hot*.

All her professional reserve was gone.

"I thought we were talking," he murmured against her lips and worked a hand under the hem of her sundress to cup the bare skin of her hip. His elbow hit the gear shift but he barely felt it.

She gasped as his thumb slid under the waistband of her panties. "Keep going and I'll lose the ability to speak entirely."

"That seems like a fair trade."

He shoved his hand deeper under her dress. His fingers hit damp heat and it was heaven. He lost himself in it, in her mouth, in her soft moans of pleasure.

He mouthed his way down the pale column of her throat and had just enough working brain cells to mutter, "Where is this headed, Ju? If you're going where I hope, this car's not the place for it."

"Mmm."

Which was no answer at all, but as her hands were inside his shirt, tracing intense, sizzling patterns on his back, he wasn't prepared to split hairs about it. He'd take whatever she gave and stop when she said stop. Worked in his favor she wasn't much of a blabbermouth at the moment.

He took them both deeper and satisfied himself by touching and kissing whatever he could get his hands on while she was still agreeable to it. Dr. Cane might repossess this delicious body at any moment.

"Shay?" She drew back, hair all mussed from his hands in it and her face shimmering with passion. "About all the changes. You did well."

All of a sudden, it hit him and he didn't need a psychology degree to figure out her miraculous change of heart. He hadn't broken through her professional barrier. Not at all. She'd finally gotten what she wanted—her watered-down, throttled-back version of Shay.

Before he could process his reaction, his phone beeped. Fishing it out, he glanced at the text message and swore. It was from Cal Blankenship, GGS's chief operating officer. The top suit. He opened it, though he knew what it was going to say. The black letters swam as he read them.

One of GGS's major contracts with the government expired soon and another company had jumped into the bidding war. It was a big, big problem. That contract kept GGS in the black and if they lost it—well, they couldn't. The company wouldn't survive.

Grant would have crushed this problem like a used paper cup and Shay never would have been involved. He swallowed against the sharp knife to the back of the throat. Nothing he could do now but see what unfolded.

"Do you need to go?" she asked.

"Yeah," he lied.

Okay, it wasn't really a lie. He needed some space from the throbbing vibe and the convoluted woman, which, combined, were too powerful for this closed-in vehicle.

She leaned in to speak, soft and low. "My room overlooks the pool and I've been thinking about trying out the spa. Maybe you'd like to join me later and give me some more to consider?"

Apparently he *had* proven that Juliana was still hot for him. As long as he was standing still.

Shay intended to skip the spa.

Yes, Juliana wanted him. But not as is. She wanted a safer version of him. Knowing he hadn't been able to rattle her enough crawled up and down his last nerve like metal on metal. All he could remember was sitting in her dorm room eight years ago, leg aching inside that heavy, uncomfortable cast as the woman he loved shredded his heart.

You have to stop, Shay. This time it was a broken leg. Next it could be your neck.

This is who I am.

Then you'll have to be you without me.

Now, pretending to watch TV, he lay in bed, determined

to keep his mind off the woman waiting for him outside, under the stars. Every channel irritated him and his attention wandered.

He lasted about thirteen torturous, imagination-fueled minutes. Juliana was down there all wet and gorgeous and he was up here, alone with his principles.

So Juliana was finally getting what she'd wanted back in college. But she wasn't handing out ultimatums. She wasn't even asking him to slow down for herself, but for Mikey. It was a different situation than before. They weren't in love with each other and he wasn't falling for her again. She was the last person he'd ever trust.

Besides, he had zero intention of permanently changing anything.

He leaped off the bed and told his conscience to shut up before it found a reason why the spa was a bad idea.

Don't think. Do.

Quietly, he let himself out the back door, opened the new gate and strode past the infinity pool to the upper level where the attached in-ground spa spilled its water into the larger basin below. The spa gurgled merrily in the midst of its flagstone housing but the lights were off, cloaking Juliana in the darkness.

"You made it," she said and her voice floated across the open space, inviting him closer. "I was getting lonely. Thought I'd be considering all by myself."

"Don't let me stop you." He halted at the stone edge surrounding the spa. Juliana was on the opposite side, neck-deep in the dark water. "Can I turn on a light so I don't miss anything?"

A splash of water slapped his bare feet in response. "Come on in, the water's fine. Not too hot, not too cold."

"Oh, too bad. I was hoping you'd ask me to warm you up." He shed his shirt, vacillated about his board shorts, but left them on until he got a better feel for what type of evening she had in mind. A kiss and a summons to a late-night pool party didn't mean she'd come prepared to put her money where her mouth was.

He had, though. Eternally optimistic, he'd stuffed a strip of condoms in his pocket.

He slid into the water onto a submerged concrete ledge across the circle from her, wincing as the salt water found the healing scrape below his knee. Weak starlight bathed Juliana's beautiful face and his lungs contracted.

"Ju, come here," he said, eager to taste her again before his earlier doubts changed his mind.

She sliced through the water and he snagged an arm, pulling her into his lap, one leg on each side of his hips. A little bikini covered all her interesting places and he was gratified to see the top tied up around her neck. Perfect.

He traced her mouth with a fingertip and replaced it with his lips. Gently, at first, but then she shifted restlessly in his lap, sliding against his erection, and he groaned.

Deep in her mouth now, tongues tangling, he nestled her closer, wallowing in the simultaneous shock of heat and cold water.

He bent his head and nuzzled her shoulder, then worked his mouth across her wet skin up to her throat, nibbling and teasing until his lips snagged the dangling string of her top.

A quick pull with his teeth and the bow slipped apart. She squeaked in protest, but it was too late. Strings fell from her neck and the two triangles peeled away to reveal rosy-tipped breasts he'd never forgotten.

Her hands flew to her top, trying unsuccessfully to cover her naked flesh.

"Ju, stop," he murmured, and gently drew her hands away to look his fill. She was still the most beautiful woman on earth.

"Someone might see," she hissed. "We're not exactly hidden."

"The staff's quarters are down the hill." He jerked his

head to the left. "The only one at the main house is Maria and she's watching Mikey via the video monitor from the media room. Which has no windows. What'd you think we'd be doing down here, anyway? Shuffleboard?"

In response, she tipped her head forward and kissed him, hesitantly, mouth sizzling on his. *Yes.* His body lit up, craving her touch, craving her heat. He tilted her head and took charge. Tongues crashed, tasting and thrusting. She was sweet like warm honeysuckle.

Still lost in her mouth, he made short work of removing that scrap of a top and let it float away in the water. Her breasts filled his palms, wet and hot.

The familiarity of her rushed back, full-force, and eight years vanished. He was twenty-two again, desperate for her, desperately in love with her because when they were together he always had a safe place to land.

His heart lurched and skipped a beat.

Oh, man, he would have sworn he was over all that.

Ruthlessly, he crushed the squishy feeling spreading dangerously fast behind his rib cage and pulled her closer to ravage her breast with his lips. It wasn't enough to stop the flood of the past, the bite of pain. He had to squelch the longing for the future he'd once envisioned with Juliana, where she accepted him as is and loved him anyway.

But she'd destroyed that dream and shattered his ability to trust her. Neither could ever be reclaimed.

All that was left was the heated vibe that still thrummed between them.

Don't think. Don't remember. Feel.

His hands roved over her curves, caressing the smooth lines, plunging into her intimately. "I want to be inside you. Now, Ju."

It had to be now, so he could immerse himself in the rush of release, the fullness of his body's carnal reactions.

This was about sex at its basest level. And that was all he'd ever let it be.

* * *

Juliana shuddered as Shay's tongue wrapped around her nipple again. Her body was on fire, her desire like a geyser, pushing toward the release of a century's worth of pent-up pressure.

That was a heck of a hot flush.

It had been *so long* since she'd been touched like this, as if every inch of her was exciting and beautiful. So long since she'd had sweaty, chest-heaving, shockingly X-rated sex.

Not since Shay.

She and Eric had enjoyed a nice relationship in the bedroom until infertility had robbed her of the ability to think of sex as pleasurable and made her believe her body was flawed. Shay had been part of her life before that had happened and might be the right man to reverse those lasting effects.

He sucked at her breast, flicking his tongue against her sensitized flesh, and she thought she'd come out of her skin. Then he took the other breast in his hot mouth, and a groan ripped from her throat.

His hands. Oh, yes. His hands burned across her skin, weaving a wizard's spell on the rest of her body.

Madness. Shay was pushing her toward insensibility and she could barely form coherent thoughts. She'd fooled herself into thinking a grounded Shay meant a safe Shay and that wasn't necessarily true.

This second chance wasn't supposed to be so crazy, so irrational. Being with Shay should be pleasurable *and* manageable because he'd changed. For Mikey. So why was Shay still so potent, so frighteningly overwhelming? Why did she still feel like she was teetering on the edge of a platform, about to leap into the abyss?

Shay gripped her bikini bottom and ripped it away, his impatience evident in the rigid bulge grinding into her flesh. After a quick wiggle, his own suit disappeared and they were skin to wet skin, his heavy length against her bared center.

Oh, my.

Shay's hot mouth claimed hers, his tongue stroking with luscious, firm pressure, sending those lovely long liquid pulls through her abdomen. Involuntarily, she arched, scooting deeper into his lap. He began exploring. His fingers delved and dipped, driving her further into a swirl of sensation that left no room for anything but the here and now.

Awkwardly, she scrabbled to grip his powerful arms before she could drift away, but he was a step ahead and steadied her with a hand to each hip.

"Be still," he said. "I have to put on a condom."

Oh, that didn't sound pleasant. Water and condoms didn't mix. Her brain was fuzzy enough to address it out loud. "You know you don't *have* to."

His hopeful gaze caught hers and held. "Are you saying we don't have to use protection?"

"Infertile. Remember? And I've had enough tests over the years to know I'm safe the other ways, too."

But that didn't mean he was.

Clarity came back in a rush. *Way to kill the mood, Dr. Cane. Why don't we trot out Shay's colorful sexual history for laughs?* She should have kept her mouth closed.

"You mean all those late-night trips to the drugstore in college were for nothing?"

She snorted at his injured expression. "Well. Not nothing. The anticipation made for some pretty good times, if I recall."

His gaze heated and a slow smile that was all Shay bloomed. In one move, he stood with her in his arms and sat her on the edge of the spa, legs dangling in the water. And suddenly, her naked body wasn't submerged any longer.

"I can't lie," he said. "The thought of going au naturel is the most erotic thing ever and I am really, really on board with that."

As the evidence was straining up out of the water, begging for her attention, she certainly couldn't argue. Or take her eyes off of it.

With one finger, he tipped up her chin and cut into her with his infinite green eyes. "I haven't slept with anyone without a condom. You only have my word, though. I would understand if you didn't want to chance it. I have a whole string of condoms, which I will use if you say so. Or not. It's your call."

Oh, goodness.

He *had* grown up, grown into an amazing man. He was willing to put Mikey first, sacrificing his own interests, and even in the heat of the moment, he took time to be sure they were squarely on the same page when she'd suggested no condom in the first place.

Above all, he obviously held a tender place in his heart for their past. He must be recalling that heightened, delicious anticipation as well.

After years of utilitarian coupling and the destruction of a marriage due to her infertility, enough was enough. There shouldn't be any barriers between her and this man, who wanted to share a special experience with her, one he'd never had with anyone else.

That was the man she'd fallen in love with.

A man she could easily—safely—fall in love with again now that he'd taken her advice to slow down.

"No condom. Just you."

With a splash, he knelt in the water and kissed her until she writhed under his mouth. Shay remembered how to touch her, yet had a few new tricks. He was relentless and thorough in pleasuring her, until his name gurgled from her lips in a plea. A prayer. A warning. She didn't know. It was all too much.

Finally, he bent one leg up and slid into her, to the hilt.

He inhaled sharply and moaned her name.

Hot and thick, he filled her, and she sought the release he'd built her toward. Urging him on, she squirmed closer, scraping her bottom on the hard stone beneath it.

He began to move, each thrust driving deeper, stretching her impossibly further. Shoving her closer to the elusive edge.

Did she want to back away? Or fly?

"Juliana," he growled through gritted teeth. His eyes were closed, lids shut in tight wrinkly lines. "It's… No condom. Very sensitive. I need you to—" He blew out a breath. "Hurry."

Her cheeks heated. "Well, we're outside and the ground is scraping me."

It was, but that wasn't the entire issue.

Shay grabbed a towel, flung it around her shoulders and hustled her out of the pool area. When she stumbled on the stairs to the second floor of the house, he swept her up in his sinewy arms and carried her to his bed.

He dropped her onto his soft, fluffy mattress and stood over her, eyes blazing, gloriously, beautifully and wickedly naked. He was indeed a centerfold fantasy, every woman's dream, with a muscled, tapered body he knew how to wield.

And she wanted it.

He crawled up her length and slid a thigh between hers, hard muscles exquisite against her skin. "Inside. Mattress. Anything else?"

"No," she whispered.

Instead of picking up exactly where they left off, he trailed hot, openmouthed kisses down her torso and opened her legs to continue at the juncture of her thighs.

Oh. *Yes.* Her back arched as he pleasured her. Her body ignited, the glow sweeping across her skin, filling her, driving her deeper into a dark void of pleasure.

Then he got serious, mouth and fingers working simultaneously. A splintery, sparking heat swept outward from her center, traveling across her fevered flesh. He went deeper and she strained closer to his mouth, losing all sense of time and place, spiraling faster and faster.

A second later, he rose up and drove into her, retreated

and plunged again, lifting her hips with his strong hands to meet his thrusts.

"Come for me, Ju," he murmured.

His thumb brushed her sensitized button and she squeezed her inner walls.

"That's it," he encouraged. He held her in place, and his strength and persistence almost undid her. The chaos swirled through her mind, sucking her down, reaching for her.... She squeezed again, tighter, and set off a lovely ripple of a climax.

Shay shuddered with his own release and collapsed against her, clutching her tight to his slick chest, wordless. She was too floaty to say anything. It was so beautiful, to lie here with Shay and be content.

Eventually, he kissed her forehead. "Next time, invite me to join you in bed instead of the spa."

She rolled into him and clung, the things inside her too big for words. A few tears leaked out and he drew back to look at her with concern.

"What's going on?" he asked. "Are you having second thoughts?"

"No, no. It's…" *The sacrifices. The changes. The sex.* She swallowed. "Thank you. For everything."

He laughed. "You're welcome. I just might keep you around. You're good for my ego."

"Then I probably shouldn't tell you, but this is the first time I've…you know…in a long time. I wouldn't want you to get a swelled head."

"There you go talking in code again. As gorgeous as you are, I don't get why you're so repressed. You didn't use to be like that."

Repressed? She wasn't repressed, though she did get a tingle at Shay calling her gorgeous. "I don't talk in code."

"You do. You couldn't even come right out and say, 'Hey, let's get naked in the spa. See you at eight for sex.' Instead, it's 'I was thinking we should talk' and 'considering' and 'you know.'" He traced her bottom lip with one fingertip and it sparked across her mouth. "Something wrong with your vocal cords? What is 'you know'?"

"Orgasm." Heat climbed into her cheeks.

"No wonder you thanked me." His grin was entirely too self-satisfying. "Glad to be of service. I expected you to say it's the first time you've had sex in a long time. Which is also good for my ego, by the way. How long is a long time?"

"Eight years."

He sat up. "You haven't had an orgasm since me? What was wrong with your ex?"

He wasn't you.

She didn't say it. There was such a thing as too much confession and Shay was one disclosure away from strutting around like a rooster as it was.

"Nothing was wrong with him," she said. "We had a civilized marriage and got along very well."

He snickered. "So he was boring."

The assessment was uncomfortably close to the truth. She'd deliberately sought out a steady, quiet man, because Shay's kind of whole-body sex was too overwhelming. It still was. "I'm not hashing out my marriage while we're lying in your bed."

She didn't want to think about her marriage. Oh, it was so evident now. She'd married Eric because he wasn't Shay. For penance, she couldn't talk about sex and she had trouble making her brain shut up long enough to lose herself in pleasure. Shay was too much of a gentleman to mention it, but she also hadn't reciprocated…using his mouth on her.

Dear God, she couldn't even *think* the correct words for that.

"You brought it up. What did he do to get you in the mood? I bet I could top it with one hand tied behind my back. Hey, that sounds interesting." He waggled his eyebrows.

"Stop," she insisted. "He's no longer a part of my life. You don't have to turn this into a competition."

"My darling Juliana, there's no competition and even if there was, I already won. Why didn't you say anything?"

"As you pointed out, it's hard to talk about."

And she didn't know how to psychoanalyze a solution. But she had to. After what Shay had given her, what he'd given up, she owed him.

He'd changed his entire lifestyle. She could at least make a couple of changes behind closed doors, right? For once, she vowed to be enough for him. She had to be or the possibility of a second chance would wither and die.

"You don't have to talk. Sleep."

He patted the pillow and she gratefully sank into it.

Seven

Mikey's wails woke them bright and early.

Shay popped one eye open and sought the video monitor to verify the baby was awake and maybe conjure some fairies to flutter across the room to take him out of his crib. "I start to question why I waited so long to hire a nanny."

"Maria," Juliana mumbled and snuggled deeper into his side where she fit nicely enough to attract the interest of his half-formed erection. "Let her go to him and you stay here."

"I gave her today off because she watched Mikey last night."

"Are you sure you're a rocket scientist?" She rolled to peer at him, hair spilling over her shoulders. The sheet slipped down to reveal one pale breast covered in light abrasions from his whiskers. "Because I'm seriously questioning your intelligence right this minute."

And now it was a fully-formed erection.

"Well, I dropped out of MIT and the last rocket I worked on exploded. So I guess that's your answer."

"Shay." Her eyes filled with raw tenderness.

He looked away. Anything remotely emotional was not something he wanted to deal with this morning. Or ever. "Go back to sleep. I'll take care of Mikey."

Quickly, he threw on clothes and disappeared from the room before she could protest. Hopefully his exit hadn't seemed like as much of an escape to her as it had to him.

Mikey's face was screwed up in a sob when Shay got to the crib. Murmuring, he scooped up the bawling lump and changed him, scoring a record one mishap with the wall beside the changing table taking the sprinkling.

Shay cleaned up, then mixed formula and, with the baby in hand, dropped into the rocking chair. Mikey sucked the bottle dry in no time and screamed for a few minutes, but settled down pretty fast compared to normal. The new formula was better, but the reflux wasn't completely gone.

With the baby quiet and snuffling against his shoulder, Shay's conscience started in on him.

Last night had been a bad idea. A mind-blowing, stellar, really bad idea.

One he wanted to repeat as soon as possible.

Juliana did it for him, like no one else, in so many ways. The smell of her lay heavy on his skin, both arousing and infuriating. In his misguided youth, he'd given himself to her completely, loved her so fiercely, that when she'd called it off, he'd physically hurt for days. Falling in love with Juliana again was not happening.

Sex was about the body and love was about the mind. He had no doubt he could separate the two, had been doing it easily since she'd left him. But could Juliana? Not so much.

And that was the problem.

He'd hoped to send her back to New Mexico in a few weeks with nothing more than some fond memories, but the look in her eye this morning had crumbled that hope into fine dust. It hadn't occurred to him that she would immediately jump to the conclusion that this relationship had legs. That she might fall in love with this watered-down version of him.

It was like Mikey's book, the one about the mouse and the cookie. If you give a girl an orgasm, she's going to want a white picket fence to go along with it. A white picket fence and a happily-ever-after.

Shay rocked harder and Mikey squeaked. Hard to tell if it was a squeak of complaint or enjoyment. Better to err on the side of caution. He slowed down.

Everyone wanted him to slow down.

Well, Juliana could want a white picket fence until NASA sent a manned mission to Pluto but that didn't mean she'd get it. His fences were iron and he liked them that way. He hadn't made her any promises. They were adults having some fine adult interaction and nothing more.

If she got attached, too bad. She could figure out how to put her smashed heart back together. Just like she'd forced him to do eight years ago.

He stewed about it while playing with Mikey. Then he half participated in a virtual meeting in his Halo collaboration room, which should have garnered his full attention since the meeting was about the new blood gunning for GGS's government contracts. Without Grant's expertise, Shay was it. Except Grant's death hadn't miraculously produced negotiation skills in Shay any more than it had gifted him with parenting skills. He hated not being able to fill the gaps.

It wasn't until Cal Blankenship called him on his preoccupation that he let last night go.

He and Juliana should clarify a few things—like the fact that there'd be no fences in their future—prior to ripping each other's clothes off again. Well, he'd done all the ripping but she hadn't complained.

With his attention on the meeting, it soon became painfully clear he'd be spending a few days in Fort Worth with the other executives working out a strategy to grind his competitor into the concrete. They'd already finessed the numbers until they cried but GGS had little room to change their current bid. It was do-or-die time.

Shay topped off his supremely bad mood later that day by preparing the Hayabusa to go to its new owner.

He loved that motorcycle. He loved all his vehicles, all his planes, loved every moving thing he owned. Other men collected baseball cards or women. He was a speed man. Or he used to be. Now he was a father and only the hope Mikey might one day share his interest in fast machines consoled him.

Shay returned to the house from supervising the shipper as he loaded the Hayabusa into a trailer, and congratulated himself for successfully avoiding Juliana all day.

She was waiting for him in the living area and when he shut the French door, she sprang up as if she'd just gotten caught with the pool boy.

"Hi," she said and stared at him with big eyes.

"Hey."

They stood in uncomfortable silence and it sucked. Now they were all weird around each other, and it was all his fault. He needed to apologize for his disappearing act this morning.

Visions of white picket fences danced in his head. So he didn't apologize.

"I talked to Emily, Donna's nanny," he said. "Interview's tomorrow and if everything works out, she can start immediately."

"Great."

She shifted from foot to foot and redid the clip in her hair a couple of times while he listened to time crawl. "Is this the part where we talk about the weather?"

"Um, I need a favor," she said and cleared her throat.

"Which is?"

"I, uh, didn't know it'd be so difficult to articulate." She took a deep breath and motioned him closer. "You're too far away and I feel like I'm shouting."

He took two steps, close enough to get a whiff of her fresh scent. His lower half sprang to life, primed from last night and primed by the soft feminine curves within arm's reach.

"So," she said. "I have a problem."

His eyebrows flew up and the organs in his chest ground to a halt in the way only a conversation with a woman he'd just slept with could accomplish. "You do?"

"Yes. It's hard for me to talk about…" Another deep breath, which lifted her gorgeous breasts, reminding him of what they tasted like. "Sex."

"That problem." He took his own deep breath and let it out slowly. Sex he could talk about all day long. Their relationship, the future or fences, he could not. Not right now, while he was still a little raw.

"It's because I have a problem with sex in general."

"Didn't seem so last night." And now he was thinking about how spectacular no-condom sex was and how long the trip to Fort Worth would be.

"Because you were doing all the work and took me along for the ride. My attempt to seduce you was awkward at best. I have no idea if I even do the right things. Things you enjoy. And I want to. I feel self-centered letting you handle everything."

Before his head could completely explode, he threw up a hand. "Wait, when did you try to seduce me?"

"In the car. When I kissed you." She looked so miserable, he couldn't help himself. He clasped her hand and rubbed her thumb.

"Ju, the car was the right thing and I enjoyed every minute of it. And every minute of last night. Why are you beating yourself up?"

"You left in such a hurry this morning and I haven't seen you all day. I assumed you were avoiding me because it wasn't so great. I want to be enough for you. In bed. You deserve that." She stood on her tiptoes to look directly in his eyes. "After a lot of thought, I have the answer. Let me try again."

Guilt had driven him from the bed, not disappointment. Worse, he'd been so determined to shut off everything but his body, so determined to wring every ounce of pleasure from the experience, he hadn't paid enough attention to *her* needs. *Idiot.*

His mouth opened to start the long overdue apology and clarify the lack of any white picket fences—because it was the right thing to do—but she kept going.

"I need...*want* to be more involved in the entire act."

He shook his head. "What are you talking about?"

"Sex," she said with a small nod. "I want sex. With you. And I want to talk about it, with the actual words, by telling you what I like. Ask you questions about what you like. Sexually."

His vision was going gray and his legs ached with the effort not to surge forward, right into her and all that wet heat. "You want to give me a survey?"

She blushed, a gorgeous stain of red that heightened her porcelain-doll features. "Not in a clinical setting. But I suppose it might be similar. I'd prefer to experiment in the moment by moving a certain way and then asking if you like it. So, it's a very logical way to solve both problems at once."

"Experiment. On me. Sexually." How he choked out actual words was beyond him.

"Please. I know it's a—"

"Shut up, Ju. Just shut up a minute." He didn't know whether to laugh or cry and if she kept babbling, he might do both. Not even the wounded expression on her face could blast through the lust-hazed vision clouding his senses, of her naked, mounted on top of him, head thrown back in ecstasy as she rolled her hips. "Sorry, I'm still trying to process."

"I know." She stared at the floor, refusing to meet his gaze.

"Infertility…well, because of it, I lost the ability to have a normal sexual relationship. I can hopefully be different with you, maybe due to our history. You make me feel things I thought I'd never feel again. In turn, I want to do the same for you."

She was serious about getting over a problem she'd developed during her marriage and she thought only he could help. That pleased him no end. And her self-prescribed therapy included talking dirty to him while she tried to figure out what rang his bells, which amounted to winning the lottery in his book.

This was all about sex. For Juliana, too.

Nobody was dreaming of white picket fences and nobody was going to get hurt.

And *nobody* could turn down a request from a woman to be the subject of her sexual experimentation. He wasn't even going to try.

"How's right now looking for you?" he asked with a grin.

She blushed again. "Last night, you said something about getting me in the mood. If you do that, I'd feel less self-conscious. I don't think I can just start, right now, with no lead-up. Maybe later tonight?"

As horrendous as this day had started out, things were looking up. The empty spot in the garage where the Hayabusa used to be parked wasn't even haunting him anymore.

Then he remembered and groaned. "I have to go to Fort Worth. For a couple of days and I can't put it off. I have to leave in an hour because the jet is booked for tomorrow."

She looked so disappointed, it cheered him right up.

"You can't reschedule?"

He bit his tongue and didn't remind her he owned a perfectly good helicopter, but *someone* had begged him not to fly it.

"Emily's interview is tomorrow, too. I scheduled it all at the same time." He took her hand and kissed it. "It's all good. Anticipation makes for some pretty good times, if I recall."

* * *

Shay had been gone for forty-eight hours and Juliana felt the keen lack of his energy every second.

He was due back from his business trip sometime tonight. Juliana tore her gaze from the clock and resituated the baby in her lap. Story time was not going well. Mikey was fussy and refused to sit still. He'd learned to crawl and that was far more interesting than the colorful circus book she'd selected.

Of course she couldn't go with Shay to Fort Worth and she'd been happy to stay here and take care of Mikey. She'd enjoyed having the baby to keep her company. They'd strolled Shay's property together and Juliana had introduced Mikey to bubble baths.

A fresh-out-of-the-bath baby smelled better than anything, including devil's food cake.

"Mikey, look at the lions. Lion," she repeated and pointed to the cartoon drawing.

He butted her chest with the back of his head and squirmed out of her lap. She let him beat the floor with his fist a few times and then she pointed to the book, which he ignored in favor of blowing spit onto his arm. She laughed. Babies were so easily entertained.

Mikey had never minded story time before. Perhaps his reflux was aggravated or his gums hurt.

"It's story time," she said. "Very important for vocabulary and communication skills. This is what time we read every day."

She pulled him back into her lap, but he screamed and wiggled until she propped him up in a sitting position, legs crisscrossed. Still not interested in the book. Maybe another one would do the trick.

The third time he crawled off the bright quilt she'd spread on the floor of his room, she gave up and let him explore the painstakingly baby-proofed room. He wasn't crawling so much as scooting, but he got where he wanted to go.

Soon he'd be walking and saying his first words. Like *mama*. Except who would he say that to? Tears pricked at her eyelids. Poor baby. Shay loved him, of course, but a mother's love was special. She wanted Mikey to have that.

He picked up the circus book and stuck it in his mouth. Definitely teething. She removed it from his grip and he yowled. Quickly, she replaced it with a soft, flat truck designed for teethers and made a mental note to buy a few more safe toys for Mikey to gum.

Mikey flung the truck at the wall and screamed. Something rose up in her throat, thick and suffocating. She should be *better* at this. And she really couldn't blame her lack of parenting skills on Shay's brain-drain any longer.

Donna would have known exactly what to do—was Juliana destined to struggle with Mikey, with babies, because she didn't share that motherly, solidified-in-the-womb bond?

God, she was a mess. Why couldn't she spend time with Mikey without doubting herself? She loved babies. She loved the idea of being a mom. But she wasn't Mikey's mother and day-to-day parenting was so much harder than she'd ever imagined.

Maybe that was because she wasn't anything more than an infertile consultant.

In desperation, she grabbed the musical toy she'd bought at the store in Fort Worth and pushed the button. Mozart spilled from the hidden speakers. It would have been nice if it instantly quieted Mikey's wails but it didn't. The concerto soothed her, though. Music had come easily, naturally, and she missed feeling proficient at something. She closed her eyes and breathed. So she would figure out how to become proficient at parenting.

Her cell phone rang and she glanced at it. Shay. Her pulse skittered as she answered, "Hello?"

"I can't wait to see you." His voice warmed her ear, low and beautiful.

She shivered and her frustration over Mikey transformed into a big ball of nerves. And something else. Anticipation. "Oh, were you gone? I didn't notice."

His chuckle swept through the line. "I got you something in Fort Worth. Something I'd like you to wear. Will you?"

"Wear it where?"

"Tonight. For me. It's something I like and you didn't even have to ask me about it."

The dreadful ball of nerves and anticipation heated. And spread.

The experiment she'd developed to solve her issues was logical. But she was scared to death. What if she tried and she still wasn't enough for him? He was just so…Shay. So physical and sensual and confident.

"Are we going somewhere?"

"Not this time. We're having dinner here. Part of my end of the bargain."

Getting her in the mood. Desire uncurled low in her tummy. He hadn't even done anything and she was already halfway there.

"I'll wear it." Out of curiosity, if nothing else. "Will you bring it to me when you get home?"

"It's bad luck to see the subject before the experiment. I brought Emily with me. Come down and meet her. There's a bag on the kitchen counter for you to take back to your room."

"You're here already? With Emily?" The anticipation-and-nerves cocktail swirled and heightened to a new, fine pitch.

"I asked the pilot to fly fast. Scold me later."

The phone went dead.

Juliana shook her head and pocketed the phone. She didn't want to think about where this was headed. Not now, not while everything with Mikey still felt so precarious. Not when she was so unsure if she could be enough for Shay. It almost seemed easier to take things slowly, let their second chance evolve naturally. Less scary that way.

Be brave. She squared her shoulders and collected Mikey, then went downstairs to the kitchen. A cute-and-bubbly brunette sat at the table to the side where the staff ate meals. Emily and Maria were chatting amicably.

After the introductions, Emily asked to hold Mikey. She hugged him close, while Mikey gurgled and waved a fat fist in Emily's face.

Juliana's stomach twisted. Mikey and his nanny were obviously fast friends.

That was good. Exactly what she and Shay had discussed. The nanny wasn't a stranger. Emily appeared to be in her early twenties, a good age for bouncing back from sleepless nights. Juliana and Shay could focus on the reason she'd come to his house—teaching him to be a father. Everything was on course.

She just hadn't expected to suddenly feel unnecessary.

Or like she selfishly wanted Mikey all to herself.

You should be the nanny, Shay had said. Casually, offhandedly. It echoed through her head at odd moments. Like now.

Ridiculous. All those years of school. All the work to build her practice, to partner with her clients, to heal and provide hope for a healthy mental future. All that traded away for a job changing diapers and pushing a stroller?

Her heart thumped once, painfully.

Nanny wasn't the job she wanted. Deep in her heart, in a place she didn't dare examine, she feared she'd begun to want a completely different, impossible role in Mikey's life. *Mother.*

Shaking it off, she smiled and went about assuring herself the new nanny was everything they'd hoped. With Emily here, Juliana could distance herself from Mikey, from all the feelings that rose up when she held him, and concentrate on her job.

Emily answered every question Juliana shot at her with confidence and wisdom. Of course. Donna wouldn't have hired anything less than an excellent caregiver for her child.

And neither would Shay.

The mysterious bag sat on the counter, large, red and unmarked. Her curiosity eventually got the better of her. She excused herself and snagged it on her way back upstairs, holding it closed up both flights of stairs to her room.

She dumped the contents on her bed. And blinked. Not a dress.

Lingerie.

She picked up the filmy, see-through scraps of silk, one in each hand. A miniscule bra and panty set. Shay wanted her to wear *this?* To dinner? Her cheeks heated.

He'd never bought her anything like this in the past. She couldn't put her finger on what felt strange, but when they'd been together before, Shay had had little to give except words and he'd given those generously. This time around, his mouth spent far too much time on her skin to form sentences. How did he feel about her? Why did he seem so reticent with his emotions?

She shook her head—after all, who'd directed emphasis toward the physical? Not Shay.

Then she saw the note: "Take a long hot bath and think about me. Wear whatever you like over the things I like. Dinner is at six in my room. Shay"

A jasmine-scented packet of bath salts had been in the bag as well. She fingered it and had to admit a bath sounded nice and relaxing.

Dinner in his room could be interpreted a million ways. She chose to assume he intended to keep their liaison low-key and invisible to the staff, which she appreciated.

When she sank into the warm slippery bath, she lay back and closed her eyes, content to do exactly as Shay suggested— think about him. Unabashedly. He was a beautiful specimen of man, long-limbed, with a sprinkling of hair across his cut torso and rough-tipped wizard's fingers. A glow flared to life in her abdomen and traveled outward at a leisurely pace, tightening all her muscles deliciously.

The heavy scent of jasmine curled through her brain like a smoke cloud and she let it.

By the time she drained the water, the lingerie didn't seem so bad. Shay had picked it out. It would be under her dress. What could it hurt?

She slipped on the bra and panties and couldn't resist peering at her image in the mirror. Not too shabby. Maybe not pin-up material, but the cobalt-blue scraps pushed up her breasts and dipped brazenly low on her abdomen. She pulled on a sundress and redid her makeup. Shamelessly sexy lingerie gave her a boost of daring, so she fixed a couple of chips in her toenail polish and left her feet bare.

At six, she went down the hall to Shay's bedroom. As she knocked, she realized she wasn't nervous anymore. She felt beautiful, pampered and desired, all before she'd even laid eyes on the man.

Oh, yes, Shay was good and she would repay him if it killed her.

Eight

Shay answered her knock, filling the doorway with an over-dose of that vibrating masculinity. Stravinsky played in the background, low and seductive. She missed hearing music inside her skin, the way she had in college. She missed the abandon of it. The abandon of being with Shay.

"Welcome home," she said and squealed as he whirled her inside. His hard body pinned her to the shut door and he took her lips in a savage kiss. His thigh wedged between hers and the friction ignited the yet-to-fade glow from the bath.

She kissed him back, shoving her hands through his hair and knocking the cap from his head. She melted against the delicious body holding her. The rub of silk against her breasts and between her legs was wicked.

He clamped her jaw with both hands and pulled back enough to lock gazes. "Turns out getting you in the mood isn't specific to just you. I've been going cuckoo waiting."

She had to smile. "Here I am. What's for dinner?"

"Does it matter?"

"No. I'm actually not very hungry."

The green of his irises flamed as he slid a fingertip under a strap of her dress to caress the blue scrap of fabric under it. He ground his thigh deeper against her. "I'm dying to see this on you. But that's not on the agenda yet."

"What is?"

He swept her over to the cozy living area of his room and sat her down on the leather couch, then picked up a short, thin glass filled with pale liquid and handed it to her. "Tequila."

"You want to do shots?"

"It's a game." At her frown, he laughed. "Trust me, will you?"

He laid out simple rules for his drinking game. He would say a word and she'd have to repeat it. If she said it without laughing or balking, he'd take a drink. If she couldn't say it or hesitated, she had to drink. And the words were obscene, unladylike and thoroughly titillating.

Clever. Shay was very, very good.

By the third sip, it got easier. Before long, Shay was drinking more than she was, and after a while, she started offering up her own words. None of it had any meaning anymore and they were just words.

She'd never have thought of this. The glow he'd kick-started spread, fogging her brain. Or maybe that was the tequila. She didn't care. Shay was beautiful and wonderful and she wanted his hands on her.

So she told him so. And he did it. But not quite like she envisioned.

"Here. Put them here." She moved his palms to her breasts and circled them over the fabric of her dress.

The music—strings and flute—throbbed around her, melding with his touch. Reminding her of before, when they'd been in love. There'd always been music floating through the air then, from the CD player, her violin. From their mouths as they moaned in euphoria together and whispered the things in their hearts.

She wanted music in her soul again. She wanted to feel connected to Shay, like he belonged to her alone, like in college.

Her head lolled back against the couch and then she couldn't see Shay, so she swung a leg around the other side of him, mounting him like she had in the spa. Her dress rode up as he resituated, nudging her already wet center with a very stimulating bulge.

"So we're moving on to the next item on our agenda?" he murmured as she threaded fingers through his shaggy, unkempt hair.

His voice was ragged and raw and it thrilled her.

"If the next item is you naked, then, yes."

She yanked on the hem of his shirt until it pulled free and let her fingers do the walking, all over the hills and valleys of his gorgeous, sun-browned chest. He watched her with his molten-green gaze, and she didn't have to ask if he liked the way she touched him.

But she wanted him to do more than *like* what she was doing. She wiggled off the couch and helped him out of his clothes until he was naked, then climbed back into his lap, straddling him. His erection was splendid and she'd barely started.

Emboldened, she whipped off the sundress and revealed Shay's gift. His eyes darkened as they swept her body, drinking in the sight of filmy silk over her feminine parts.

He reached for her but she shook her head. "You may look but not touch."

"I thought the point was to do stuff I like," he rasped. "I like touching you."

"No, the point is for me to pleasure you." Her speech was a little slurred, but gravelly and seductive, even to her own ears. Tequila was wonderful. She loved tequila. "By doing things you like. While talking to you about it."

To demonstrate, she rocked her hips against his, rubbing silk against his erection. That felt so nice, she did it again, and circled her pelvis. Waves of heat rippled from her center, arching her back involuntarily. She shivered.

He groaned, deep in his chest, and it vibrated through her thighs. "You're batting a thousand so far."

This was supposed to be about his pleasure, not hers. Not yet. "Well, I'm going for two thousand."

She slid off the couch and knelt to use her tongue in the most inventive way she could envision—dragging it up his flesh from base to tip. He almost came off the cushion and scrabbled to grab hold of it, knuckles white and eyes shut. "Do that again and this will be a very short experiment."

"Wasn't planning to do it again."

Instead, she nibbled the tip into her mouth and sucked. He strangled over unintelligible syllables. She refused to let him pull away. He protested feebly and she ignored him, exploring with her tongue and her lips, using high pressure, low pressure, studying his reactions. His eyes never left her face.

He tasted delicious, wild and free. Or maybe she'd projected that into the experience because it was how she felt.

His fingers tangled in her hair and he came in a rush and fell back, rib cage heaving.

That had been amazing to watch. Why hadn't she done this before? She had caused a strong man like Shay to tremble and come apart.

"My turn."

Shay hauled her back into his lap and stood with her in his arms, easily carrying her to the bed. Gently, he laid her down on the comforter and worshipped her with his eyes. Amazing how beautiful he could make her feel, simply by looking at her.

"Should I take this off?" She reached for the bra's clasp.

"Absolutely not."

He fell onto the mattress and rolled her into his arms, then laid his lips on hers in a soul-stealing kiss, a silent bit of communication that spoke volumes. *Feel this,* the kiss said. *Feel me,* the man said. She curved against him, seeking his warmth, hands roaming over his body, never touching enough to satisfy herself.

He took her deeper into the kiss, drugging her with his heat, his vibrancy. Her thoughts fragmented and she couldn't gather all the pieces.

His mouth trailed down her throat to her breast and his tongue dove beneath the silk to capture her nipple. *Oh, yes.* Rough and insistent, he laved her as his fingers dipped lower, curving inside her panties. A finger slid into her wet heat, and she writhed, whirling into the black place where chaos lived.

Instinctively, she started to draw away but Shay held her close. Held her tight as he took her higher. She squirmed, arching against him. His fingers performed magic against her fevered flesh.

Music swelled with her arousal, crashing through her body in dual stimulation, amplifying the whirl. Nothingness beckoned, urging her to fly into it.

It should be easy, to just fall. Why was it so scary?

"Stop," Shay murmured. "You're thinking so loud, I can hear it. Look at me."

She did and her pulse sputtered. His eyes were dark with passion, bottomless. Magnificent.

He lifted a hand and kissed her fingertips. "You are beautiful. Sexy. Everything about you is gorgeous." He kissed his way down her arm to the curve of her elbow and glanced up, eyelids at a sensuous half-mast. "You taste divine and smell even better. It's not, and never could be, a chore to spend time making you feel good."

Her heart squeezed and when it let go, warmth flooded her body.

"Shay," she whispered. It had always been Shay.

"Don't think." He settled between her legs, opening her thighs and kissing them. "Watch me. Feel what I'm doing to you."

His lips touched her through the damp silk and she felt the pressure, the heat, then his tongue burrowed around the barrier, building the tension, spreading the heat. Somehow he knew exactly what she needed, exactly how to touch her. Her mind drained as he drove her to senselessness.

"Watch me," he commanded and rose up, fingering the silk aside to enter her. "Does it look like I'm disappointed?"

Rapture dominated his expression as he slid out and slowly pushed back inside. She felt every millimeter of the contact, every shade of desire on his face. Felt her own responses keep pace with his. It swirled in her head, blacking out her vision for a moment.

"It's just so much," she said with a shuddery warble.

"Yeah. So much. It's amazing. So good." He inhaled deeply. "I could live in this feeling forever."

He circled his hips, driving deeper, and her lids fluttered closed. It *was* good. Amazing. His fingertips grazed her sensitized flesh and the pressure built. He'd always plunged her into a place of pure sensation where logic and order disappeared. For the first time, she wanted to let him take her there.

She could live in it forever as long as Shay was there, too. As long as he never left her behind.

"Tell me what you want," he said.

"More," she blurted. *More of everything.*

He responded instantly, diligently, and the black, slippery slope of the chasm called its siren song, begging her to soar up and away from the edge. Begging her to feel and forget whether any of this made sense.

"Ju?" She looked up at him. He was so beautiful and so patient. "There's nothing wrong with you. Whatever this experiment was about, it's not necessary. You turn me on every minute of every day."

Her heart broke open and spilled all over everything. She was lost.

"Ride the wave," he whispered and she did, embracing the chaos because it was Shay, and she couldn't touch the ground, and that was okay because he would catch her.

The void claimed her in a roaring crescendo as Shay claimed her body. She stared into those deep green eyes she'd never forgotten and plunged into them.

Lost. And found.

Everything coalesced in perfect harmony. She burst with a dozen rapid contractions and took him with her. All the colors of the rainbow exploded in her head, in her body, lighting up the darkness, banishing it. Her body bowed with the force of the ricochets and finally relaxed as the symphony of background music washed over her.

Shay was wrong. The experiment had been absolutely necessary because *something* had shifted. It had never been like that. She would have remembered.

It had never been like that. Shay would have remembered. And never let Juliana out of bed.

The whole point of dinner in his room had been to set expectations. It was sex, not a date, like they were a couple with a future. He'd get Juliana over her weird idea that he didn't enjoy sex with her and in turn, she'd blast him into orbit a few times.

It would have worked like a charm except for all the problems it caused. Somehow, when he was deep inside her, the line blurred between body and mind. Between sex and love.

None of it seemed very separate, at least not when he looked into her eyes. Each time they made love, the line got a little blurrier. Hence the problem.

Instead of dwelling on it, all through breakfast, he relived last night. In full color, superb detail, over and over, because wow. The first night had been spectacular. He'd chalked it up to not having been with a woman for a while. Last night had bordered on an out-of-body experience. He'd chalk that up to sending Juliana's inhibitions out the window.

There was the cause of all the line-blurring. He'd just gotten a tad bit emotional over how great the sex was.

Juliana glowed this morning. Beautifully. Dangerously. He could hardly concentrate on spooning oatmeal into his mouth.

Oatmeal. Sawdust. Same thing.

It certainly couldn't keep his attention off the gorgeous woman across from him, who was chatting with Emily as if she hadn't had her world completely rocked. How did she do that?

She glanced at him with a secret smile he had no trouble deciphering and his never-quite-dead erection blasted straight upright. Yeah, so she'd rocked his world, too.

He was really fond of no-condom sex and really, really fond of tequila, especially if it led to Juliana's mouth on him like it had last night. Reliving that several times in a row made the oatmeal taste no better, but he didn't mind so much.

Suddenly, breakfast was over. Juliana pushed back from the table and Emily collected Mikey from his high chair. Emily had adapted easily to the new household, falling into her nanny role with no trouble. Mikey responded well to her and Shay appreciated the break from the middle-of-the-night scream sessions. With a sunny smile, the nanny disappeared, Mikey in tow, leaving Shay and Juliana alone. Finally.

"You coming, Shay?" Juliana asked and he blinked.

"Not yet, but I will be shortly if you want to experiment on me some more."

She blushed and smacked him on the arm, dousing him with her scent. "I meant are you coming with me and Emily on Mikey's morning stroller ride?"

That scent short-circuited his brain. Every time. "Yeah, I'll go. In a minute."

He pulled her into his arms and backed her up against the wall for a good-morning kiss. As a bonus, when he kissed her, that white picket fence in her eyes wasn't visible.

The less he thought about Juliana's fences, the better.

She opened underneath his mouth and he fell into her. His hand was halfway under her dress before he realized they were in the dining room.

"Later," he promised and released her.

She nodded, eyes smoldering and dark, and cleared her throat. "Okay."

He followed the two women into the yard and trailed the stroller until Emily parked it under a large Globe Willow. She spread a quilt and let Mikey crawl around on it. It was pretty great to watch him explore, chubby legs and arms moving.

Juliana lounged on the quilt, laughing at the baby. A slight breeze knocked a lock of hair off her shoulder and his fingers curled automatically. He wanted to plunge them into that hair, pull her head back and do many more wicked things. Let her do some wicked things back. Except they were outside, with the baby and Emily, in full sight of the house during broad daylight.

He'd have to wait to sink into her again until this evening. He glanced at his watch. Geez. How many hours had they added to the day when he wasn't looking?

Mikey crawled toward Juliana and fell face-first into her lap. She picked him up and repositioned him to crawl in the opposite direction, her hands capable and gentle on his body. She was so good with him, more patient and caring than he'd had any right to expect from a consultant. Mikey loved her, too, and responded to Juliana every time like he had from the first moment.

One day, Mikey would be walking and Shay had trouble

swallowing. Juliana wouldn't be here to see it. It seemed wrong.

Well, the camera on his phone worked, didn't it? He'd send her pictures.

Juliana beamed at the exploring baby, beautifully framed by the green grass and clear sky. Shay's chest squished in that way he'd thought he'd banished to the nether reaches of the Andromeda galaxy.

Danger.

Enough of this homey little scene. Emily was here, doing her job, and he had a lot of work to do. He dropped a kiss on Mikey's fuzzy head, made his excuses and left without a backward glance.

But the image of the baby and Juliana together wouldn't fade from his mind's eye, no matter how many screens he opened on his laptop. It didn't help that behind the image of his kid and his lover stretched a hundred-foot-high white picket fence.

Juliana hadn't said a word about fences, white or otherwise. He was the one who kept freaking out because he didn't know what was going on in her head. After last night, the look in her eye probably had more to do with their fine adult interaction than anything.

Maybe if you gave a girl an orgasm she really just wanted another one to go with it.

Which was perfect. Exactly where both their heads should be.

The meeting in Fort Worth to develop a strategy for retaining their chief government contract had not gone well and he needed to focus on work, not Juliana. Somehow, he needed to pull a Houdini on GGS's budget, which was not his forte. But he had to figure it out.

Lunchtime came and went, but he didn't realize it until Juliana poked her head into his home office. Sometime in the past few hours she'd twisted her hair up into a clip, Dr. Cane-style.

"I brought you a sandwich," she said. "Would you like it?"

A glance at the clock told him it was near two. "Are you going to feed it to me?"

She wrinkled her nose. "No, I'm trying not to bother you."

"Sure. That's why you brought me the sandwich instead of sending a maid."

"I'm not used to being waited on hand and foot like some other people I could mention," she informed him pertly. "Bothering a maid never occurred to me."

He grinned and leaned back in the chair, stretching his back muscles, which were not so thrilled to have been hunched over a desk for hours. "I'm not complaining. You can bring me lunch anytime."

She entered the room and set a plate on his desk, along with a bottle of soda. Aha. She finally remembered what he liked to drink. Or the cook had told her, which was more likely. And why did that realization disappoint him?

"I had an ulterior motive," Juliana confessed and his eyebrows went up.

"I'm a really big fan of ulterior motives."

Before she could protest, he swiveled and hauled her into his lap for a thorough kiss. She sagged in his arms, molding to his chest, and he fitted a hand against her waist, holding her in place to better access her gorgeous mouth. The things that mouth could do. There was something superhot about Dr. Juliana Cane on her knees before him, like she had been last night.

When he drew back, her lips and cheeks were stained pink and dang if the clip from her hair wasn't in pieces again. She wasn't so calm and professional now, was she?

He seriously enjoyed rattling her. When she forgot to think, when she let herself go, man, she was something else.

"I really came to talk," she said breathlessly.

"Mmm." He took her lips in another deep kiss and yanked her dress down to palm a breast through her bra. Not his favorite one, but Juliana's rosy nipple was inside, so he liked it pretty well. He'd like the bra better off but she pulled on his hand, protesting.

"Really, Shay. Now that Emily's here, I'd like to spend two hours a day on our lessons." He nuzzled her throat while she talked, turning her speechless. Unfortunately, it didn't last long. "I was hoping to get a firm commitment. What does your work schedule look like?"

"Awful." He straightened her dress but didn't let her move from his lap. She smelled too good. "I intended to take an extended leave of absence while you were here, but some unforeseen circumstances have intruded."

"What's going on?" She smoothed a lock of hair from his forehead, concern drawing her eyebrows together.

"One of my competitors is throwing his weight around, making noises about a lower bid on one of my government contracts." He shrugged, making light of it. "It's stuff Grant used to deal with."

"I'm sorry." She laid her lips on his in a butterfly kiss, as if she knew how hard the whole mess had been on him. She probably did. She'd always been good at reading him.

"Thanks." He shut his eyes as she leaned into him, wrapping her arms around him in silent comfort, wrapping him in Juliana and he breathed it in. She soothed him and he sorely needed it.

"Tell me about it."

The suggestion was so easily given, so unobtrusive, he did.

"It's a nightmare, being the one left holding all the pieces. We were good together, the three of us. Grant was the brains. Donna, the heart. I can't recapture that. It's gone. They're gone and GGS will never be the same."

He clung to her as his throat filled.

"Shay," she whispered against the hollow behind his ear,

and her essence bled into his skin, warming it. "I'm here for you."

That strength was exactly what he needed, what he'd always needed. From her alone. She was still his safe place, still beckoning him home with her warm, eternal landing lights. No matter what else might be going on, this hadn't changed and he clamped on to it tightly. His lungs shuddered in his chest.

She clasped his face in her hands and kissed him gently. "Grant was the brains and Donna was the heart. What are you, Shay?"

He didn't want to say it, couldn't say it. Her perceptive gaze said she'd already figured out the answer. Because she saw through him, easily, and always had. "You can put away Dr. Cane. It doesn't matter."

"Right now, with you, I'm just Juliana. And it does matter. Say it, Shay. Otherwise, it will stay in your subconscious and you can't acknowledge its validity. Say the word and hear it. Internalize it."

He blew out a breath. "Courage."

And she was on target 100 percent. Saying it aloud gave it weight. Truth.

Courage. The concept uncurled inside him, reminding him of how it felt. "I'm the one who talked Grant into dropping out of grad school. Donna had designed this sweetheart of an engine with the lowest heat signature in existence for a class project. Grant showed it to me, all excited. I saw dollar signs and knew we had to move fast. I was right. That engine ended up in the first ever suborbital spy plane."

"Yes. You have vision and the guts to turn it into reality. A rare combination. You're the bravest person I know. Hang on to that and you'll find your way."

It seemed so easy. With the scent of Juliana flooding his senses, more seemed possible than had moments ago. But she didn't know the worst part.

So he told her. "When the prototype exploded, it was during the second test. The first one—that's the one I had to be in." Always blazing the trail. Always first in line. "But…the engine wouldn't catch. It was a scratch. We had a deal. Me first, Grant and Donna second. The second one is the one that exploded. Why didn't I do the second test, Ju? They had a son, a life together. What do I have?"

"You can't do that to yourself." She shook his shoulders for emphasis. "You can't dwell on the past or ask why. They made their choices, not you. They didn't have to get in the ship and they didn't have to let you go first. Why did they?"

"They knew how important it was to me. Space has always been my dream, to conquer it—tame it. To create the possibility for anyone who wants to see the vast reaches of the cosmos firsthand to do so. And for that arrogance, I might lose the company. It's floundering without Grant and Donna, and I'm not enough to steady it."

"Yes, you are," she stated calmly, as if it was a fact. "Fight for it. You've got a couple of brain cells yourself. Who came up with a drinking game to help me through a stupid phobia about saying 'orgasm' out loud? I have a psychology degree and I'm not smart enough to come up with that."

"Well, I was motivated. I did enjoy watching those words come out of your mouth. Say some right now."

She didn't smile. "I'm not letting you change the subject. You're intelligent and you've also got a huge heart or you would have jumped at the chance to ship Mikey off to his grandparents. Don't let guilt cloud you. Find that extra dose of daring you've got and live up to the S in GGS."

Her firm faith shoved his pulse into double time. The warmth of her body against his, the conviction radiating from her gaze, centered him, giving him the foundation he needed. She was right. He'd always thrived on things that scared the hell out of him because if he was afraid and didn't charge ahead, then fear won. Fear couldn't be allowed to control him.

If he gave up the space tourism initiative, really and truly gave it up, a part of him would wonder forever if he'd done it because it was unsafe or because he was afraid.

He'd never run from a challenge. He couldn't start now.

Nine

Juliana divided her days between writing notes and passages for her book, spending time with Emily and Mikey and imparting parenting expertise during her sessions with Shay. She tried to focus but feeling like she didn't have all the answers when it came to Mikey slowly leeched her confidence with the book.

Her nights were wholly Shay's, which didn't help her focus.

By unspoken agreement, they were discreet about their nocturnal activities. They didn't go on dates or flaunt their relationship. They didn't go upstairs at the same time and disappear into Shay's bedroom. He didn't hold her hand in front of the staff—but he never hesitated to pull her into a shadowy alcove to kiss her breathless, if the timing was right, and his sense of timing was uncanny.

Shay fed her thirsty soul with beautiful notes of pleasure. She couldn't get full of him, couldn't stop the flood of longing for these moments to last forever.

Every night, she got ready for bed by washing her face and

taking off her clothes. Instead of donning a nightgown and reading by lamplight like she used to before falling asleep, she slipped a robe over her brazen nakedness and snuck down the hall to Shay's bedroom.

Most of the time, they didn't make it to the bed. For the first round, anyway.

Tonight, she barely crossed the threshold before his mouth landed on hers and his impatient fingers pushed the robe away. By now, his hands knew her body so well it took mere minutes to shove her off the cliff. She fell willingly and he followed.

Later, cocooned in his sheets, she lay there, drifting, listening to him breathe. He was safe and whole, and thanks to her suggestions, would stay that way. In the silent aftermath, it felt an awful lot like they were lovers in every sense of the word. Were they?

Something always stopped her from asking. Eight years ago, he'd told her often that he loved her. Especially when they were joined, he'd whisper it as he connected to her very core with nothing more than his soulful green-eyed gaze. Then he'd say it again, afterward, as he cupped her face and kissed her.

Everything was different this time. *He* was different. Quieter and more apt to hesitate before he spoke. It bothered her.

Maybe it was simply that they were different people now. More cautious about making promises. She had a life in New Mexico, clients she loved. A meaningful practice she'd built herself. Shay had his own life and a new son, who had a nanny now and didn't need her. The consultation period was almost over and they'd never discussed what might happen when she completed the terms of their agreement.

A sharp tug of longing to be a part of the family she'd helped create rose up in her throat.

She wasn't in a position to be talking about next steps. It

made good sense to evaluate her goals and what she wanted from this relationship before Shay swallowed her whole again.

So it was good that he wasn't talking about tomorrow or the next day.

"Hey, Ju?" Shay's hand came up to stroke her hair. "Why didn't you and your ex adopt?"

She filtered the out-of-the-blue question, unsure how to answer. It wasn't the first time he'd mentioned Eric directly after they'd made love. Was he worried about his position in the weird man-competition in his head?

"We talked about it. At the beginning, when we first started in vitro. If it failed, we promised each other we'd move forward with our lives together. That didn't work out."

"Why not? You always said you wanted till-death-do-you-part, preferably with 'death' happening in fifty years. I almost choked on my coffee when I read you'd gotten divorced."

Why not? It was a good question. "I didn't set out to get divorced. The whole process of in vitro is difficult and we drifted apart."

"You filed though. Not him."

She sat up. "Thorough, aren't you? Yes, I filed because I wanted it done. Eric brought it up and then backpedaled. What are you getting at?"

"Lie back down," he advised mildly. "I was going to say that even with good intentions, some promises can't be honored."

He was all sexy and disheveled with the sheet down around his waist, but instead of burrowing against his chest like she had been, she settled into a cold spot on the other side of the bed.

"I didn't mean to break the promise. But you can't imagine what it was like to go through four failed rounds of IVF."

"No, I can't. But I do know what it's like to want something. Isn't that the basis of it? You wanted a baby."

"I did. More than anything." A small piece of bliss she

could carry in her womb, nurturing it to maturity, and then give birth to a miracle. "I know the science. Females have a drive to procreate, but when you're in the middle of it, it's all pure emotion. I—I couldn't handle it."

Her voice hitched and Shay scooted into her cold spot, eliminating the distance, gathering her up close, like she'd held him the other day in his office. The sheer purgatory of those years rose up and slowly spilled from her mouth.

"*In vitro* is Latin for 'in glass.' And that's how I felt, like I was behind this glass wall and nothing could reach me. Not Eric, not my clients, nothing. I wanted a baby so badly."

Even now, she couldn't explain why the need for that life to be growing inside her was so strong. She wanted to be a mother and it trumped everything else. Mikey's sweet face and precious baby noises churned up all those feelings again, and the difficulties she faced in caring for him added an extra layer of distress.

The ghost of that baby she'd never conceived still haunted her dreams. It would have been a girl, or at least she imagined it would be. A girl with her blond hair. Their connection would have transcended birth and Juliana's purpose in life would be fulfilled. She'd be closer to making up for the lack of parenting in her own life.

Shay's fingers against her neck silently encouraged her to go on. "I was distracted all the time, couldn't remember simple things. I burned dinner to a crisp almost every night. Cried over missed phone calls and cotton commercials on TV. But every time I called for the results and some disembodied voice told me I wasn't pregnant, I didn't cry. I couldn't."

Tears slipped down her cheeks in a slow waterfall as she again traveled through the seven levels of infertility hell.

"Other women were getting pregnant and I wasn't. It made no sense, had no quantifiable outcome. And it was so unfair. I couldn't control anything. Eric gave up trying to reach me. I didn't argue."

"God, Ju. I'm so sorry." Shay's lips grazed her temple and held there for a long time. "I'm floored to think of you being so frazzled. You probably scared the bejesus out of your ex. You're normally so composed. I had no idea it was so difficult for you."

"No one does," she whispered. "Not even Eric."

She'd never shared any of the internal anguish with Eric. She shut him out as surely as her womb had shut out the fertilized eggs. Her skin went clammy.

She'd shut him out because she hadn't been in love with him.

"But you told me."

She had. The last thing she wanted to do was examine why, but she'd done a lot of avoidance where her marriage was concerned. Maybe now was a good time to take a hard look at the decisions she'd made in the past eight years, a lot of which had to do with the man holding her.

"With you, I can be Juliana, not Dr. Cane. I've never had that with anyone else," she confessed. It was a connection she'd never realized had so much value. "I'm supposed to be the healer, not the wounded, so I keep a lot inside. I'm not good at sharing."

She wasn't even good at analyzing the things she kept inside. She'd married a man because he wasn't Shay. A man she hadn't loved.

"I know. Most of the time you're a complete mystery to me."

"I am?"

"It's part of what's so fascinating about you. You're never boring."

That was a revelation. She'd been certain Shay would grow tired of her after a while. He wasn't afraid of anything and she had no idea how to have his kind of courage. No idea how to be enough for him unless he wasn't moving at the speed of light.

He stroked her hair again. "You know how I told you I'm adopting Mikey. Do you think it's the right decision?"

Oh. That's why he'd asked about her and Eric's decision not to adopt. Gratefully, she latched onto the subject change. "Absolutely. It's important for children to feel wanted, which adoption will foster."

He flipped to face her, searching her expression. "Ju, I own a company responsible for manufacturing morally question-able machines. Agents of war. The military isn't buying my planes to transport daisies. You don't think it's a bad idea to adopt a kid under those circumstances?"

"Security isn't morally questionable. Everyone wants to feel secure and you're facilitating that in an honorable way. It affords you a great opportunity to sit Mikey down in the future and have a conversation about the sacrifices required to keep our country safe. There's nothing wrong with pro-tecting the way of life you hold dear."

He nodded. "Write that down. You might be telling it to the judge. I found out today that's the Greenes' main argument against me since I've dropped the space tourism initiative."

She shook her head. "Is that where all these questions are coming from? What a ridiculous objection. Mikey's bio-logical parents helped build those planes, too. Don't let the Greenes plant doubts. You're already a great father and you'll only get better."

Shay. A great father. As unbelievable as it would have been at one time, it was true. And uncomfortable. She'd once thought Eric would be a great father because he drove the speed limit and bought organic food. There was so much more to successful parenting, like sacrifice and commitment. Shay wore those qualities like a second skin.

"Some of the doubts were already there." He made a face. "Do you think it's possible to love an adopted child as much as a biological one?"

"Yes, if you stop thinking of Mikey as an adopted child."

The words came automatically, as if counseling a parent
These types of questions were common and easily answered
"He's real, Shay. As real as a child you fathered the natural
way."

"Could *you* love an adopted child as much as the one you
thought you were getting out of those petri dishes?"

She let the words echo through her brain. Through her
heart.

Yes. She already loved Mikey, more than she should.

Her eyes burned. Love wasn't the only component to good
parenting. She'd pushed Shay to hire a nanny, not because he
needed one, but because *she* needed one. The distance she
thought would help her do her job was really a way to avoid
facing the fact that she wasn't enough for Mikey. She wasn't
his mother, and she never would be.

Once, she'd weighed the future of her relationship with
Shay against whether he'd be a good husband and father—and
he'd come up short. Now she was the one coming up short.

"I don't know how to answer that," she whispered.

I wouldn't know how to be the parent he needs.

And until she knew, she had no business longing for a second chance with Shay. Or thinking about Mikey as anything
other than Shay's son.

A few days later, Boyd and Karen Greene arrived via the
car Shay had sent to the airport. They emerged and Shay
walked down the front steps to welcome them. He instructed
the driver to take the Greenes' suitcases to the guest quarters.

The Greenes eyed Shay and he eyed them right back. Shay
had been best friends with their son for a decade, and they'd
spent many family holidays together. Usually Shay had accompanied Grant for moral support since he and his father got
into it every time. Shay and the Greenes had eased into a wary
tolerance of each other, despite Mr. Greene's intense dislike
of the friend who had encouraged his son to drop out of MIT.

Of course, that had been before the explosion, for which Mr. and Mrs. Greene placed the blame squarely on Shay's shoulders.

They looked even older and more impossibly withered than they had at the funeral.

"Did you have a nice flight?" he asked and wondered how long they would exchange pleasantries before the gloves came off.

"Yes, thank you," Mr. Greene responded as Mrs. Greene clutched her husband's arm. "We appreciate the invitation. It was unexpected."

Shay inclined his head. "My fault. We shouldn't be strangers. Mikey is your grandson and I want you to be a part of his life."

Mr. Greene glanced around, taking in the expansive property. "Our lawyer thinks you've invited us here to talk us into dropping the custody petition. He advised us not to come."

Grant had shot straight, too, something Shay had always appreciated about his friend. It was unfortunate Shay couldn't find common ground with his friend's parents.

"We couldn't do that," Mrs. Greene jumped in, her eyes bright and imploring. "Nothing could have kept me from Mikey. Where is he?"

"In his room with Emily, his former nanny. I hired her to work for me."

Mrs. Greene clapped. "Oh, I love Emily! She's so good with Mikey."

Shay blessed Juliana for suggesting he contact Emily. No, he hadn't invited the Greenes here to talk them out of the petition—he wasn't losing custody whether they dropped it or not. He'd fight these people in court until he ran out of money, which would take a very long time indeed.

But he did want to foster a long-term relationship with them and if they approved of Emily, fantastic. Mikey should know all of his biological family, including Donna's parents and their surviving teenage daughter, as well as all of his adopted family. Hopefully, Shay could do it well enough that Mikey wouldn't distinguish between the two.

"I'll show you around," Shay said.

The Greenes followed him inside the house and up the stairs to the nursery. Mrs. Greene rushed into the room and scooped up Mikey. A mistake. The baby burst into tears and tried to squirm away. His grandmother's face fell as she handed him back to Emily. The nanny soothed him with quiet murmurs until he reduced the volume to tiny mewls.

The air shifted and Shay didn't have to look over his shoulder to know Juliana had appeared at his back. He could sense her like a wolf knew his mate. He liked thinking of their adult interaction as exactly that—mating. Not emotional, not squishy, just fierce animal coupling he could not get enough of.

Unfortunately, he had a sneaking suspicion wolves mated for life. As he had once dreamed of doing with Juliana.

Her hand rested on his arm and slid up to his elbow where it fit comfortably. A designer suit clung to her curves, and man, did she wear it well. His tongue nearly stuck to the roof of his mouth.

"I'd like to meet the Greenes," she said in a low voice drilling straight through him.

He introduced them, identifying Juliana as a child-rearing expert he'd hired to acclimate him to fatherhood.

Such a short phrase to encompass the sheer backbone and generosity she brought to the job. She'd overcome a difficult bout with infertility and emerged with a drive to help others. A weaker woman would have given up, would have refused to be around children in any way, shape or form.

"You're surrounded by hired help," Mr. Greene noted. "Do you do anything yourself or do you just wave your money around?"

Shay declined to bite. After all, their son and daughter

in-law had been wealthy and now, so was the baby. Shay had the wherewithal to protect Mikey's money as closely as he protected the kid. Few people could claim the same.

"I do what's in Mikey's best interest."

Mr. Greene sized him up. "If that was true, you'd see it's best if we get custody."

"We disagree," Juliana interjected smoothly. "Shay is an excellent father and I'll testify as such in my capacity as a child psychologist. Grant and Donna trusted him. Everyone else should as well."

Well, hell. Now she was turning him squishy when they weren't in bed.

The Greenes stared at Juliana, but she didn't blink and he was glad to have those composed blue eyes on his side.

Mrs. Greene snapped her fingers. "You knew Grant and Donna. At SMU. I thought your name sounded familiar. I have a picture somewhere of the four of you."

Juliana smiled graciously. "You have an excellent memory. I hadn't seen them since graduation, but yes, we were all friends then. Mikey's had enough excitement. Will you allow Shay to show you to your room? I'm sure you'd like to freshen up after the flight."

Slick. In one shot, she'd increased her credibility with the Greenes by asserting a prior relationship with Grant and Donna, then arranged to get the older couple out of his hair, giving him a chance to regroup.

Juliana was so hot when she was all authoritative and professional and in charge.

Especially when he knew exactly how to rattle her out of it. When he was the only one who could.

The Greenes nodded and Shay ushered them from the nursery.

The second he extracted himself, he cornered Juliana in her room. He shut the door with his foot. Startled, she looked up from her desk, hair all prim and proper. That was about to change.

He advanced on her, hungry to get under that professional suit she'd donned, likely in anticipation of meeting Mikey's grandparents. Her expression darkened as she took in his.

"I guess I don't have to ask if this visit is business or social," she said.

Without bothering to waste energy on words, he hauled her out of the chair and plunged in. Their bodies slammed together, then their lips, and he devoured her mouth, desperate to taste.

To feel her under him.

To mate.

To possess.

He wanted her naked and completely undone. Rattled, exponentially.

When it was untamed like this—when *she* was untamed, her moans drowning out the sound of ripping cloth—it was better than anything he'd ever experienced. An unparalleled high.

He loved it when she abandoned herself to pure emotion, pure sensation. Loved being the one to get her there. Loved knowing this woman who could hold the weight of the world on her shoulders could handle whatever he lay on her.

Her hands sparked across his back, trailing luxurious fire, heating him to the boiling point.

He tore his mouth from hers and lifted her breast, sucking the nipple between his teeth. Her head fell back and she arched, pushing more of her sweet flesh between his lips. With a small nudge, he pressed her against the desk, lifted her thigh and sheathed himself inside her.

His skin and bones vanished as he synthesized with her and they became one. So beautiful, how easily she accepted him. No resistance, just unadulterated pleasure. So hot, and so sinfully decadent.

Now for his favorite part. "Talk to me, Ju."

With her erotic murmurs of encouragement washing over him, he pistoned his hips, slowly, then faster, surrendering everything to her. She absorbed it, reveled in it with soft gasps and moans. That fresh Juliana scent invaded his senses. His blood raged through his veins and his body howled for release.

Not yet. It was too good to end.

"Touch me," she commanded in a tight whisper.

"You, too."

His fingers twined with hers, guiding her to the apex of where they joined and they pleasured each other until the seismic shocks of her dazzling climax set off his. He blasted into the sonic explosion at a million times the speed of sound.

Vision still hazy, he put his arms around her and held on. She folded into his embrace and laid her delectably disheveled head against his shoulder. Centering him. Calling him back to earth with that seductive lure, like she always had.

His chest was feeling squishy again but he couldn't withdraw. Not yet. This game was so dangerous, the one where he pretended being with her was all about sex, where he pretended he wasn't getting far too attached to Juliana.

But the danger pulled at him, daring him to face it down.

The woman in his arms had the power to make him bleed. Internally, where it couldn't be bandaged. And that was the scariest thing he could imagine.

But he would not be controlled by fear. He never had been, and he wouldn't start now.

Juliana's phone rang. She lifted her head and glanced at the caller ID.

"Oh, no." She pulled away and answered the phone naked, which revived his hard-on enough to hurt.

Jeez, was there anything she did that wasn't sexy?

The Greenes were probably all rested up and a proper host would get back to them. He gathered his clothes and then caught sight of the devastation on Juliana's face.

The phone slipped from her grasp and she followed it to the carpet, her frame boneless. His pulse flipped and missed a beat.

"What happened? One of your parents?" he asked as he knelt next to her, unsure how to comfort her.

Her eyes were glassy as she shook her head. "Amanda. One of my teenagers. A client. She tried to commit suicide."

"What can I do?"

"Nothing." Juliana pressed both hands to her cheeks and rose on shaky legs. "I have to go to the hospital. She's asking for me."

Shay dressed quickly, then helped her into her clothes. "Of course. You can take the jet. Whenever you're ready. Stay as long as you need to. I'll have the pilot on standby for you."

Out of nowhere, he almost blurted out that he'd go, too. To be there if she needed him.

For once in his life, he bit back what was on his mind and didn't offer to accompany her.

It would be difficult logistically for both of them to be gone. The Greenes had just arrived and Emily was a new employee, not ready to be left in charge of both Mikey *and* his grandparents. Or at least that would be his excuse if Juliana asked.

In reality, the distance would be good for them both. Give them a chance to evaluate. By the time she returned, he'd have a much better handle on all this squishiness.

She didn't ask.

Then he had a different thought. "Are you coming back?"

Obviously distracted, she pulled out a suitcase and started dumping items into it without looking at them. Or him. "I don't know."

His pulse missed more than one beat. "You don't have to. Emily's here now. If you want, I'll consider our consulting agreement concluded in full."

The job. He hadn't even been thinking about the stupid

job when he'd asked the question. But what else was there between them? What else could he allow?

"I appreciate that. I'll call you and let you know if I'll take you up on it." She sank onto the bed, head bowed. "I wasn't there for her, Shay. I have to get to her, to help. I don't know anything until I figure out how this could have happened."

And then she zipped the suitcase, swung it off the bed and rolled it out of the bedroom. She was leaving and might not be coming back. No mention of stocking up on white paint and fence pickets.

He waited for the gush of relief to fill his body. It never came.

Ten

Juliana perched on the cushioned chair at Amanda's bedside and wished the bandages on the young girl's wrists weren't so starkly white.

Amanda squeezed Juliana's hand weakly. "Dr. Cane. You came."

As if there'd been a possibility she wouldn't have. She'd told her clients she'd be gone for two months. Not forever. This was her job, her life. Her identity. "I got here as fast as I could."

If nothing else, her time with Shay had shown her this life was the best one for her. She was a good therapist. But she still wasn't sure she could be a good mother to Mikey. Or be a good wife. Not now. Maybe not ever.

The teenager's dark hair fell into her face as she glanced down at her arms. "I guess you know what happened."

Down to the last gory detail her parents had shared, which Juliana didn't believe for a second was the whole story. "Tell me."

The girl's eyes filled. "Troy broke up with me."

"I'm sorry, honey." Troy had been Amanda's very first boyfriend. A total loser, as established by the girl's many stories, but none of Juliana's carefully worded suggestions to that end had penetrated. "How did he do it? Text message or Facebook?"

With teenagers, the method was often the greater source of contention than the message.

"Worse. By kissing Candi Adams in the cafeteria. Right in front of me. Then he laughed and said she's better in bed than I am."

"He's lame, Amanda. And you and I both know you're too smart to slash your wrists because Troy chose a public venue to declare how much of a scumbag he is."

Amanda's grip on Juliana's hand tightened. "Okay. There's more."

Yes, there always was.

That was the reason Juliana had dropped everything, including Shay, and flown back to New Mexico. Amanda wouldn't tell anyone else. Only Juliana. They'd forged a bond over the year she'd counseled the teen, listening to her angst and drama without judgment. This wasn't her first suicide attempt, but the last had been nearly nine months ago.

Amanda trusted her. And Juliana wouldn't abandon her.

"It's that…" Amanda swallowed. "I gave him everything. He didn't like me being on the drill team, so I quit. I keep my hair long because he told me to. I didn't even want to sleep with him in the first place. Not yet. But I loved him so much I was willing to do whatever he wanted. Why wasn't that enough?"

Ah, the million-dollar question. How many sacrifices were enough? She thought of Shay and all she'd asked of him, in the past and now.

If the Greenes gained custody, would he curse himself for not making more sacrifices? Or would he curse Juliana for asking him to make those sacrifices when they hadn't worked in his favor?

"You already know the answer to that question." Juliana cocked her head in expectation.

Amanda huffed out a sigh and rolled her eyes as only a teenager could. "He wanted someone he could control, not a girlfriend."

Almost a word-for-word recitation of what Juliana had said over and over.

"If you know all this, why the suicide attempt?"

"I don't know," Amanda said sullenly. "I just wanted to be dead."

If she'd actually wanted to be dead, she would be. Amanda collected terrible grades to annoy her parents but she wasn't incapable of anything when she set her mind to it.

"Do you still wish you were dead?"

"Sometimes."

Juliana watched her silently until the girl's mouth twitched.

"I wanted Troy to be sorry I was gone and sad it was his fault."

"If you kill yourself, it will never be Troy's fault."

"You're mean, Dr. Cane." Amanda pulled her hand free and faced the wall.

Rationally, she knew the girl only lashed out because she hurt and wanted everyone else to hurt, too. Knowing it didn't stop the twist of pain from stealing her breath. The connection she shared with Amanda, with her clients, meant everything to her. She wanted to say the right thing.

She smoothed her expression to mask her reaction. "I treat you like an adult and you appreciate it. So here's an adult question for you. What do you think you could do differently in the future to have a better relationship with a boy?"

"Not have one."

"A valid choice. And also unrealistic. What's another way?"

"Don't be such an idiot over a guy who says he loves me." Amanda sat up at Juliana's encouraging nod. "I'd like to be with a guy who likes me exactly the way I am. Troy wanted me to be someone I'm not. I let him turn me into someone I don't like. Why did I do that? I sort of thought if I cut myself, I wouldn't feel so dumb about doing everything he asked and maybe he'd realize how much he hurt me."

Juliana's lids flew closed in relief. The girl *had* been listening. This wasn't a suicide attempt—it was a ploy for attention.

"Very good. You assigned too much power to Troy by letting him dictate your actions. True love is a compromise. You each bring your best and give one hundred percent to the other. It requires sacrifice and commitment."

"Yeah right, Dr. Cane." Amanda rolled her eyes. "I just want to be with a guy who makes me happy."

Happy. As a foundation for a relationship. The notion was incomprehensible.

As Juliana drove home from the hospital, her mind worked over the realization that she'd never once made a decision based on whether it would lead to happiness. Not giving up music. Not breaking up with Shay. Not marrying Eric.

All of her decisions had been based on what would logically bring the greatest degree of stability.

And even then, none of them had given her what she wanted.

Instead, she'd battled an infertility nightmare and her only support was a husband she'd shared no connection with. Isolated and alone, she'd salved her emotional needs with her clients. It was satisfying work but psychology certainly hadn't healed the damage from all that had come before.

The only happiness she'd experienced in the past ten years had been found while playing her violin or in Shay's arms. A passion she'd ignored since college, and a man she'd subconsciously distanced herself from because she and Shay didn't make sense.

No matter what she insisted, she hadn't flown back to New Mexico solely for Amanda. It had meant a good, clean break from Shay. Timely. She needed to heal before she could be in a relationship, either as a mother or a wife. And Shay was so…not the same, so closemouthed.

It had to end sometime.

Shay had learned an incredible amount about being a father, and though he had a lifetime of parenting skills to master, he'd already agreed to an early termination of their consulting arrangement—likely, he recognized the same limitations on their affair.

In short, she had no good reason to go back to West Texas, but she had a really bad one—she wanted Shay. Fiercely. Selfishly.

For once, she wanted to be impulsive and impractical. Forget about the future. Forget about not being enough for anyone and stop dwelling on the terrible consequences of chasing a second chance with Shay. She wanted to do something that felt good and made her happy, for however long it lasted.

That's what Shay was all about. What he'd been trying to impart to her since forever.

When she got home, she threw her suitcase on the bed and packed as she dialed. When Shay answered, she didn't even say hello.

"I'm coming back. Right now."

Shay would have rearranged the Big Dipper to make "right now" a reality, but unfortunately, shuffling stars was as impossible as clearing the jet for takeoff during a thunderstorm with sixty-mile-per-hour winds. Shay texted Juliana with the news it would be morning before the pilot could come get her.

Nonetheless, Juliana was coming back.

With an abundance of anticipation and energy coursing through his veins and a long wait for his midnight bed partner ahead of him, Shay didn't bother to try to sleep. Instead, he ducked out into the rain and dashed to the garage.

Once inside, he shook off the raindrops and sat at the new workstation he'd set up after Juliana had left. Most of the vehicles were gone and Mikey wouldn't be old enough for an activity worthy of an indoor space for years.

So instead of wasting all this great emptiness, Shay had converted the garage into a project center where he could escape the house and work on ideas without interruption.

Okay, not *ideas.* There'd only ever been one—safe, affordable space flight for average citizens. Space tourism.

He wished he didn't have to be so secretive, but the Greenes were still visiting and until they dropped the custody suit, he wasn't taking any chances.

Juliana had left and he'd been sure she wasn't coming back. He'd thought he'd have no reason to reveal his secret. At some point, though, he'd have to tell her he'd picked up the initiative again.

Right now, he was going to solve the fuel line problem that had caused the prototype explosion, come hell or high water.

Thunder cracked overhead and a simultaneous flash of lightning brightened the windows. He ignored it and studied the CAD drawing from a different angle. This had been Donna's forte, but Juliana's faith in him would not be in vain. If GGS's competitor came in with a lower bid on the government contract, the company would need a fallback.

Space tourism was the answer. Projections showed a large profit margin and the facility had already been built. It was a no-brainer.

And, honestly, this project room gave him a sense of purpose that had been missing since the explosion. Giving up the cars, the motorcycles, the helicopter—the entire list was too long and depressing—none of it seemed quite as bad when he hunched over this workstation, keeping his dream alive. A dream Juliana would have to understand. And accept. Eventually.

He worked until after two in the morning and finally had to call it quits when the lines on the CAD drawing blurred. The storm had abated a few hours ago and he slept like the dead until morning.

By eight, he stood on the tarmac, watching the jet taxi to a stop. Juliana appeared and walked down the metal steps, her gaze locked to his. The post-storm sky stretched wide open and blue behind her, as magnificent as the woman it framed.

The squishiness was *so* not under control. But he didn't mind so much. She'd come back and that changed things. How, he wasn't sure yet.

When she fell into his arms and he breathed her in, it didn't matter how things had changed. All he wanted was to be in this moment, this feeling of soft female against him, for an eternity.

"Missed you," he said gruffly and squeezed tighter.

She murmured in agreement and her hands slid down his back suggestively. "Let's get out of here."

White-hot need sluiced through his body as she accompanied the declaration with a blatant circle of her hips against his instant erection.

The drive from tarmac to front door took eight minutes less than normal. Juliana didn't complain. The crackle of pure sexual energy in the car could have powered the engine by itself.

He helped her out of the car, left the suitcases and dashed with her up the stairs to his room, stopping only long enough to shut the door.

They stripped each other impatiently and he boosted her up. She locked her legs behind his back as he stumbled to the bed.

"Hurry," she commanded and arched her back, shoving her damp center against his pulsing erection.

In-charge Juliana was so erotic he nearly burst then and there.

He lowered her onto the bed and surged forward, sliding into ecstasy. Her arms held him as she lifted her hips to mirror his thrusts and she murmured his name, over and over. He met her gaze, so solid and warm, and reached down between them to touch her intimately, but the intimacy was in her eyes.

He plunged into it, into her. He'd thought she wasn't coming back but she was in his arms and the heavens aligned. There was more here than just sex and they both knew it.

She shattered with a small cry, never breaking eye contact, and he surrendered to his own release.

Still locked in the throes of the aftermath, he rolled, taking her with him to settle into a tight tangle of limbs and dewy skin. Then he threaded his fingers through her hair to hold her head against his thundering heart because he couldn't let go.

All the undercurrents of their relationship, then and now, swirled into a muddle. He knew he wouldn't have called her. It would have felt like giving Juliana permission to build her fence around the Shay she dictated. Or to have his heart sliced from his chest and handed back to him on a platter if he begged her to take him as is, and she said no deal.

Neither had much appeal.

But *she'd* called *him* and now, here she was in his bed, still gorgeous and grounded but stronger from the trials she'd survived. Maybe ready to have a conversation about whether she could be happy with him long-term.

If she could love him even though he still yearned for the sky.

Maybe he was ready to give her another chance.

It was time to put some definition around what her return signified.

"I got you something," he said. He slid out of her embrace and retrieved the wrapped box from the closet.

Truthfully, he'd had this gift for weeks. There were rules.

You bought expensive presents for the woman you were sleeping with, especially when you weren't giving her anything else, like promises. But he'd been sleeping with her every night and never found the right time to give it to her. Now seemed pretty good.

She sat up and accepted the large box, shiny expectation glimmering in her expression. Did he ever like it when she dropped her impartial doctor facade and showed him what she was feeling. Rattled, times two.

The wrapping paper fell to the floor and she opened the box. She sighed and tilted her head, staring at the contents with a misty smile.

"Is it okay?" he asked, and cursed the quaver in his stomach. He'd spent a long time picking it out.

"It's beautiful." She lifted the violin from the box and held it to her nose, inhaling. "I'd forgotten how much I love the smell of wood."

"I thought you might like to start playing again. For me, if you want to."

"I'm rusty." She laughed and cradled the violin like it was a child, running a hand over the body and twisting the knobby things at the neck. "It'll probably sound more like angry chimpanzees than music. But I confess I've been thinking about playing again. It's like you read my mind. Thanks. It's a great gift."

"You're welcome." He stared down at her, naked and glowing and so utterly the embodiment of everything he'd ever dreamed of having. He couldn't breathe. "Ju, why did you come back?"

She glanced up, surprised.

"Our agreement was done," he continued. "You could have stayed in New Mexico forever. We've very successfully sidestepped the land mines of this conversation so far and I'm done dancing. You called. You came back. Why?"

Calmly, she laid the violin on the rumpled bed and crossed

her arms. "Why did you give me a violin and then ask that question?"

"I asked you first."

With narrowed eyes, she swept him with a look. "The consulting job may be done but we're not. Do you disagree?"

"No. Should I?"

"No."

"Good. What the hell did we just decide?"

"We're boyfriend-girlfriend?" She laughed and got up on her knees to put both hands on his shoulders. "Sorry, I've obviously spent too much time in the company of teenagers."

He smiled despite the fact that they'd skated around the subject again. "Is that what you want? To be a couple again?"

"No labels, not yet. We have lots of other land mines to navigate, like Mikey. And the custody suit. My practice in New Mexico. My leave of absence isn't permanent and the most I can stretch it out is another couple of weeks. I just want to be with you. That much I know."

He opened his mouth to ask, *Be with me for how long? Under what conditions? Is there a possibility of compromise?* But he couldn't get the words out. "Okay."

"Can we take it day by day for now?"

That sounded good. Day by day meant no hearts on platters or white picket fences. Her return hadn't meant something more and the nugget of disappointment wasn't hard to swallow at all. Not really. The sex was staggering. What wasn't to like?

"Day by day for now." He swept her into his arms, fell on the bed and captured her mouth with his.

After a very long minute, she squirmed away, panting. "Are the Greenes still here?"

"Yeah. Why?" He moved in to taste the sweetness again but she slapped a hand on his chest.

"Because it's 9:45 a.m. and the lack of your presence downstairs is most likely very conspicuous."

He groaned. "Okay. Get dressed and we'll go hang out with them and Mikey. They're leaving this afternoon, though, so tomorrow morning, don't make any plans."

He'd tell her about the revived space tourism initiative tomorrow. Or the next day. No point in dealing with his semi-broken promise to stay on the ground until they were both ready to talk seriously about the future.

They spent time with Mikey, ate lunch and traded long scorching glances. But all day, Shay ignored how he'd never answered Juliana's question about why he'd given her the violin and *then* asked why she'd come back.

He ignored it because the concept was so foreign, he didn't even want to put a name to it. But it rocketed through his head nonetheless.

He'd finally become cautious.

Eleven

The Greenes left late that afternoon and Juliana unpacked her suitcases in Shay's room, per his suggestion. He liked their stuff mingled. Liked her shampoo in the shower next to his. He'd never lived with a woman and doing it without expectations or time frames was awesome.

Shay leaned back in the chair of his home office and went over the new projections for the fourth time. It still wasn't pretty. If GGS lost the government contract, the company would fold in six months. A year, tops.

Their competitor's bid remained secret. His best people had been on the materials budget like white on rice and there was very little give. They could lower GGS's bid slightly. But not much. Probably not enough.

His phone rang and he glanced at the caller ID. His lawyer, Dean Abbott. Again. This custody suit was killing him. He'd really thought the Greenes would loosen up after a tour of his home, where they'd seen for themselves he had Mikey's best interest in mind.

Shay answered. "What's up?"

"You should have told me you were involved with Juliana Cane," Dean chided.

"I'm involved with Juliana Cane."

Wow. There really was something about saying stuff out loud that made it real.

For the longest time, in his mind, being with Juliana had been about proving something to her. Maybe to himself as well.

At some point the status had shifted. He'd like to say it had happened during the day-by-day discussion. But he'd be lying. They were involved regardless of the lack of labels and neither of them would walk away unscathed. The thought was sobering.

"That's a problem if we still intend to use her as an expert witness. The Greenes claim you're sleeping with her in order to influence her testimony."

Shay cursed. The hot morning love session in his room had been more conspicuous than he'd imagined. "I didn't realize I was that good in bed."

"The judge probably won't block her from testifying, but it does weaken your position. It would be better to stop seeing her for now. You can always pick up with her again later."

"It would be difficult to shield my eyes every time I get in bed. How do you think the Greenes knew we were involved? She's living with me."

Was she? In every sense? That was one parameter they'd definitely skipped when laying out the definitions of whatever it was they were doing.

When Juliana's leave of absence was up, what then? A long-distance relationship? She would live in New Mexico half the week and with him the other half? Maybe she intended to end it then.

He didn't like the sound of that.

Blindly, Shay felt behind him for the chair so he could sit in it. Except he already was.

"It's serious, then? The Greenes' lawyer spun it like you were having illicit liaisons hours upon hours of the day." Dean paused in dramatic lawyer fashion. "Hmm. How serious? Serious enough to flash an engagement ring around?"

Shay went cold. "Are you suggesting we pretend Juliana and I are engaged?"

He couldn't do that. It was too easy to picture sliding that ring onto Juliana's finger for real. He could also picture her living under his roof forever, filling the gap she'd left eight years ago, becoming his wife, becoming Mikey's mother.

But engagement rings and taking things day by day were an oxymoron. And *moron* pretty well described him if he was contemplating a conversation with Juliana about forever.

"It would be a slam dunk, Shay. If you had a fiancée in the picture, especially one who is a noted expert on child-rearing, the judge would look upon that favorably. We wouldn't even need Juliana's expert testimony."

Shay rubbed his chest, right between his pecs where the burn hurt the worst. "I don't know. I want this petition to go away because the Greenes realize I'm the best choice for Mikey. Not because I rigged appearances."

But what if the petition went away as a side benefit of marrying Juliana?

"I haven't told you the worst part. They filed to block the adoption."

Shay's vision blurred with instant rage. "What? They can't do that."

How could these stubborn, judgmental people be related to the guy who'd been his best friend for more than a third of his life?

"They can. It's a temporary block, pending the custody hearing, but it's a block all the same. The judge allowed it because if they win custody, it nullifies the adoption. The court is only looking to save themselves time and money."

"They could have saved both by rejecting the custody petition in the first place." He grunted. "I'll think about it."

He slammed the phone down and stared morosely out the window. His home office overlooked the pool but now his view was blocked by eight-foot-high iron bars.

The cold, hard truth slapped at him. He didn't trust Juliana not to break his heart again but he couldn't fathom letting her go. Not yet.

While he was at it, he might as well admit he'd been careful not to give her a chance with his heart from the very beginning.

His acquaintance with caution wasn't so new after all, not when it came to Juliana. But he'd always charged ahead in spite of his fear. This situation was no different.

Courageous. That's what Juliana had said about him.

And marrying her would solve all his problems in one shot.

As long as he could do it without allowing her to destroy him again.

Juliana checked her appearance in the full-length mirror in Shay's decadently sumptuous bedroom for the eleventh time. The azure dress was tasteful and stylish, but most importantly, appropriate for any type of evening Shay had in mind. Of course, if he'd told her where he was taking her for their first official date, then she wouldn't have had to guess what to wear.

The date request had come out of nowhere. They'd been feeling out their relationship—*feel* being the operative word since mostly they made love instead of talking. Which was fine with her. She had no idea how to do day-by-day other than to spend a lot of time not thinking, and Shay definitely assisted by keeping her naked and sated as often as possible.

Shay came out of the bathroom breathtakingly gorgeous in a dark suit, hair swept back and tame. And he'd shaved.

"You clean up well," she said, but immediately missed the stubble. His bare cheeks revealed the sharp planes of his jaw, giving him a fiercely inaccessible beauty.

"Thanks. You, too." In what seemed like an afterthought, he crossed the ocean of carpet and pecked her on the lips. "Nice heels."

She stuck a leg out, catwalk-style, to display the four-inch Manolo Blahnik knock-offs she'd bought for their first date in eight years. "These old things?"

"Later, after we get back, keep them on," he suggested, but instead of the lascivious wink she'd expected to accompany such a demand, he stared at her thoughtfully.

"Everything okay?"

"It's strange to be going on a date with you when I'm not picking you up from the dorm. We're getting dressed in the same bedroom. When we get back, it's a given we'll go to bed together, whether we have sex or not."

"Oh. I thought sex was a given, too. Are you angling for me to get you in the mood?" She raised an eyebrow enticingly. "A striptease maybe?"

"Everything you do gets me in the mood," he said with dead seriousness.

The hair on the back of her neck ruffled. They shared a bedroom, furniture. A bathroom. Occasional nighttime baby duty. She drove his Land Rover to Abilene, the closest city, at will. It had all the trappings of something that felt like more. But it wasn't, because she knew she couldn't be more for him, or for Mikey, no matter how much she wanted to. It took more than love to make a family work. Did he know she was marking time until all this disappeared?

She didn't want to ask. But had to.

"Is there something you'd like to discuss?"

He drew up her hand and kissed it. "It's different, that' all."

"Yes. But better." And then he relaxed, so she did too. He' simply made an observation, one she'd noticed as well. Noth ing to get excited about.

They talked about Mikey in the car until Shay turned dow a road marked Hamilton Planetarium and Observatory.

Oh, my. The significance hit her with a punch to the heart He'd taken her to a planetarium on their third date and as the hunched in their seats, he'd whispered to her he loved her fo the first time under the medley of stars above.

A number of significant events in their relationship ha taken place with the heavens to witness.

How had she not remembered that? He tried so hard to in clude her in his interests, in all possible ways. They'd eve made love for the first time in eight years under the canop of night and she'd been the one to suggest it. Maybe she' subconsciously sought significance all along.

He helped her out of the car and led her inside but in glar ing contrast to their third date, the place was empty of othe patrons. "I rented the entire planetarium," he told her in ex planation.

Of course he had.

She followed him into the main viewing area where th stunning panorama of stars lit a single table set with crysta and china. Dinner for two under the dome of the universe with Strauss playing softly through hidden speakers. Musi to mark the occasion as he'd done many times before.

Her knees weakened. She liked plain old Shay just fin but billionaire Michael Shaylen had a lot to recommend him

The food was excellent and the wine plentiful, served b unobtrusive waitstaff. They ate, Shay was attentive and sh kept waiting for her horse to fall off the carousel.

It did, right after dessert, when Shay took her hand an

queezed it. "I've been thinking about day-by-day and that's
ot working for me anymore."

Her stomach spasmed but she kept her face blank. She'd
nown this was coming. In retrospect, his strange mood
hould have warned her. "Are you saying you'd like to end it?"

He nodded slowly and the spasms traveled up to her throat.
Of course he'd finally figured out he needed someone better
uited to be his companion, to be his son's mother. Someone
vho had more to offer than just love.

Well, that was good. Mikey and Shay both deserved the
est.

But then he looked straight at her. "What if I wanted some-
hing more permanent?"

Permanent? Like the opposite of ending it?

The stars above spun.

"Spell it out for me, Shay. How permanent?"

"Very." He pulled a box from his pocket and flipped it
pen to reveal a flash of fire attached to what looked suspi-
iously like a ring.

Her pulse started hammering and a hundred thoughts ca-
eened through her head. But the strongest one was how the
vord *love* had never come out of Shay's mouth.

"Are you asking me to marry you? Because I missed that
art."

He plucked what had to be at least a ten-carat diamond
ing from its cushion and held it up. "Yeah. I am."

"Don't sound so excited," she blurted out before clamp-
ng her mouth closed. Her fingers scrabbled for purchase on
he chair's seat. "I'm sorry, can we start over? I'm sure this
sn't how you imagined this going and I know it's not how I
nvisioned it."

His eyes narrowed. "How *you* envisioned it? Did you know
was going to propose tonight?"

"No, of course not, or I would be handling it better. But
ou've obviously forgotten I'm a girl and you and I used to

be in love." *Used to.* Were they now? "I imagined you pro
posing to me plenty of times."

His lips pursed. "Me, too."

"Now? Or then?"

"Both. I had a ring. Back then. A gold band. It was all
could afford." His eyes speared her and her tummy fluttere

"I had no idea."

"I know." The ache spreading through the pool of gree
in his gaze said everything he didn't.

Her heart flipped over with a painful squelch. He hadn
given it to her because she'd broken up with him. And some
how, they'd found their way back to each other. Somehow
as he always did, he'd gathered up the courage to try again

"How did you think you'd propose?" she asked. "Bac
then?"

"Pretty much like this, at a place where we could see th
stars. I've been saving the idea."

Her whole body liquefied. He'd never been romantic, bu
made up for it when it counted. "I imagined you on one knee.

Solemnly, he stood, skirted the table and knelt by her chai
Her breath caught as he drew the back of her hand to his lip
and stared at her through those deep Shay eyes. "Will yo
marry me?"

Shay.

It had always been Shay, except he wasn't that same bo
she'd fallen in love with all those years ago. He'd change
He was a man with responsibilities, a business he'd built him
self, and he wanted to marry her. She didn't have to fear th
slick darkness of an uncertain future because he'd alway
be there for her.

The answer was suddenly easy.

"Yes."

They'd figure out the land mines together. They mad
each other happy and nothing else mattered. Day-by-da
had been another sort of experiment, for both of them. She'

been afraid to ask for more but Shay, who was never scared, charged ahead anyway.

Thank goodness.

He guided the ring onto her finger—it was a little big and would have to be sized, but that was okay—and then he kissed her and it was so, so sweet.

"We have a lot to talk about," she said when he pulled back. Like how selfish it was for her to say yes. "But we can wait. Can we go home?"

Home. It would be her home. And Mikey would be her son. She'd love him as much as his biological mother had. More. She'd figure out the answers to the elusive question of how to be a good parent, like she'd work out how to handle her clients in New Mexico. No clue how it would happen, but she'd take another lesson from Shay and worry about that later.

Like she'd worry about why Shay hadn't said he loved her later.

They drove back and he held her hand when he wasn't shifting gears, shooting her small, tight smiles when she glanced at him.

He took her to bed, slowly drawing off her first-date dress, and she forgot to leave on her heels, but he didn't comment. He didn't talk at all, just touched her and kissed her and it was a slow, sensuous ride of pleasure. Shay's smooth cheeks glided over her skin without that delicious prickle of stubble. Different, but still amazing.

Before she lost herself in the delirium of release, she murmured, "I love you."

She had for a long time and it was finally okay to admit it.

Eyes closed, he nodded. "Yeah. Me, too."

And then she shattered. He followed, but instead of holding her close like normal, he rolled to his pillow and stared at the ceiling.

"What's wrong?" She thought she knew. Day-by-day

had been her idea and he was no doubt worried he'd moved too fast.

"I'm sorry. You deserve a better engagement evening." He exhaled and turned to face her. "I have to tell you something. The Greenes blocked the adoption."

There was the source of his tension. She smoothed the hair out of his face and ordered her racing heart to calm down. "How can they?"

"My lawyer said it was temporary. You know, in case they win the custody suit."

"But they're not going to win."

He smiled at her fierce insistence. "They could. Just being realistic."

"We have to get married as soon as possible. The judge would never give a baby to an older couple over a young, married couple."

"Yeah. That's probably true." He looked away and a funny tickle climbed the back of her throat.

"You already thought of that. Didn't you?"

He shrugged. "We can go to Mexico this weekend. Get married on the beach. If you want."

Suddenly all the pieces clicked into place—his tension, the proposal, his response to her declaration of love.

Everything was different this time because Shay wasn't in love with her.

She'd spent the evening rationalizing away his strange mood and convincing herself of something that wasn't true.

"You asked me to marry you so you can win the suit."

The accusation dug under Shay's skin like well-placed bamboo shoots.

"I asked you to marry me because I wanted to."

Which was absolutely true. But the sour squelch in his stomach said maybe he'd used the custody petition as an excuse to avoid delving further into his feelings.

"Would you have asked me if the Greenes hadn't filed to block the adoption?"

There was no good answer to that question. But the silence probably gave her all the answers she needed.

"Were you intending to go through with the wedding?" she finally asked.

His temper flared, but he choked it back. "Of course. I honor my commitments and there are other factors besides the custody petition that went into my proposal."

Arms crossed, she stared him down. "Like what?"

This conversation was going downhill fast and he couldn't put a finger on why. Instead of a misty-eyed fiancée who was getting everything she'd ever wanted, he faced the firing squad of Juliana's logic.

"Mikey needs a mother." And he was willing to do whatever it took to give his kid a great mom. If she wanted to talk logic, he'd give her the most sensible reasons on the planet. "You're perfect for him."

"You're not in love with me. Are you?"

No. Absolutely not.

Except he was pretty sure that squishiness in his chest was more than fondness for the woman he was sleeping with, but he wasn't planning to address that now or ever. "It's not that simple."

"Yes, it is." She laughed, bitterly. "I'm not sure what's worse, that you would actually have gone through with the wedding or that you thought I'd be okay with marrying you to beat the Greenes."

Shay's temper spiked again, and he jumped off the bed to pull on jeans and a T-shirt because he couldn't stand being exposed a minute longer. "What do you want from me, Juliana? Flowers and poetry? I'll have a rose garden delivered tomorrow."

"I want you to be like you were before!" Eyes shut, she took a deep breath. "Remember how it was in college? You told me you loved me all the time. Especially when we were making love. You'd look at me with your heart all over your face. I miss that."

Fury stained his vision. This time he didn't try to rein it in.

"You miss the way I was before? Me, too. I liked that guy. I liked fast cars and rock climbing in exotic places. I liked flying and dreaming of a day when I would reach the stars. I liked being in love with you. Unfortunately, I don't get to be that guy anymore. But I get to be Mikey's father, and I thought I got to have you, too."

A nasty hot flash burned the back of his neck. Had she *ever* loved the real Shay?

Her expression smoothed out. He was standing here bleeding while she remained unaffected. This was his payoff for laying it all on the line.

"You're angry."

Did *nothing* penetrate that level head of hers? Her ability to stay composed had always been the thing he liked most about her. Right now, he wanted to see that she ached over all they'd had and lost, like he did.

He'd marry her and live with her for the rest of his life, for Mikey's sake, but he would not ever tell her he loved her again. She asked too much.

"What I've given up still isn't enough for you? You want my heart, too? Too bad. It's still in pieces back in Dallas."

Calmly, she nodded. "So this is about what happened in college."

"The past is the past. I told you I was leaving it there." Well, he was trying to but he'd pretty much failed miserably at that. "This is about the present. I did everything you asked and the Greenes are still charging forward with the suit. I don't know what else to do."

He sank to the floor, tired of being angry when Juliana had simply asked questions about their relationship—questions his subconscious had already been needling him about. She rapped a sheet around her naked torso and scooted out of ed to join him on the floor.

"Shay, the past is never in the past. We shouldn't have ried to brush it under the carpet." She pulled her knees up o her chest and locked her arms around them. "For what it's orth, I'm sorry about what happened. Then and now. But I lways did what I thought was best."

"Best for you."

She inclined her head. "Yes. I broke up with you because couldn't stand the thought of losing you, of you dying nd leaving me alone, especially not if that had happened fter we'd built a family and a life together. If I was going o lose you, I had to do it on my terms. It was the only thing could control. It's human nature to take the path of self-reservation."

"That's *your* nature, Ju. Not mine."

"Touché." Her knuckles turned white against her knees. I could tell you were struggling with the makeover. Why idn't you say anything if the changes were so suffocating?"

Wearily, he scrubbed his face, but he'd shaved and it felt ll wrong. Too smooth. He was rough around the edges and ked it.

"Because it was the right decision. I would never have nade the changes otherwise. And yet it seems to have been or nothing. Apparently the only thing that will properly im-ress the judge is if we're married. The Greenes are claim-ng we're having orgies at noon while the help watches their recious, innocent grandbaby."

"I can see the point." She stared at the wall. "The changes eren't meant to suck out your soul, Shay. I was only try-g to help. But I'll admit I liked the idea of you being safe."

Finally, the truth.

"That was pretty clear, especially after you kissed me in e garage while we were 'talking.'" One of the few times he'd had no trouble deciphering what was going on behind her blue eyes.

"Let's pretend we hadn't had this conversation, and I cluelessly pick out a white dress. We go to Mexico, get married and the Greenes drop the petition." She rested a cheek on one knee, and met his gaze. "Then what?"

"Is this the part where I tell you I'm still working on the space-tourism prototype?"

Pain exploded in her eyes but she banked it. "You never intended to stop, did you?"

The quiet accusation settled inside and was true enough to churn up a prick of guilt. "You left. I thought you weren't coming back. All my cars were gone. The Hayabusa was gone. Guess what was still there through all the painful changes? The stars."

Her lids flew closed and she swallowed. "You're still planning to get in that spaceship."

The challenge hung in the air. He could hedge. Lie. Or he could issue a challenge of his own and find out once and for all whether she wanted the real Shay or a man who didn't exist.

"I can't be permanently grounded. I'd make both of us miserable. I have to be the real me."

This is the me I want you to love.

He should have started the evening with this conversation. Then maybe they'd still be in bed instead of hashing out their relationship's past, present and future.

"Fair enough. Marriage isn't the only way to impress the judge, you know," she said decisively. "There's another option. A better one. We should split up."

And there it was—Juliana handing him that platter. Again.

But this time, he'd been smart enough not to give her the heart she'd have gladly thunked on top of it.

Twelve

"Split up?" Shay repeated. "How is that the answer?"

Juliana couldn't breathe around the shooting pains in her lungs. After admitting he wasn't in love with her and that he still planned to test the spaceship himself, had he really not seen this coming?

"Because I can't be with you. Not this way. Not even for the sake of Mikey and the custody petition."

Especially not for Mikey. Pure selfishness had caused her to say yes to Shay's proposal, along with a naive assumption Shay's love would fix everything.

Now she had to do the right thing.

Donna had loved her son enough to give him to Shay. Juliana had to find the courage to love Mikey enough to act in his best interest, too.

"But I need you to win. Would it make a difference if I was in love with you?"

He cleared his throat, likely because it had been so difficult to get the sentence out. Love clearly wasn't on the table

here, and he'd already confirmed her belief he'd only consid
ered marriage because of the petition.

Shay still wasn't the right man for her. Because he didn'
love her. Because she still wasn't enough to keep him on th
ground.

Unbelievable. She'd flown headfirst into the chasm, smac
into another broken heart. She had to pull free from Shay'
quicksand a second time and this time loving Mikey mad
it ten times harder.

"But you're *not* in love with me." He started to speak bu
she didn't let him. "I have to go home."

Her voice cracked. Mere hours ago, she'd started think
ing of *this* as home.

"Yeah, that's your specialty," he said bitterly. "Walking
away. Can you even spell the word *commitment*?"

The harsh words stung but she refused to show it. Letting
her guard down had been one of many mistakes with Shay
Hands shaking, she shook her head. "I'm doing what's bes
for everyone. You'll win the custody suit without a wife. Bu
I'll still testify if you want me to."

"Why can't you compromise? Stay. Marry me, live in lux
ury and be Mikey's mom. All you have to do is accept me.'

"I can't compromise on this." The hollowness was back
far worse than it had been at dinner. She was giving up fa
more than Shay could know. "And I don't want you to b
trapped in a marriage with someone you don't love. So w
can't be together."

She'd been right. He'd changed—into someone unrec
ognizable, someone who'd locked his heart—his soul—
away. Though he'd given up his cars and motorcycles, h
still wanted to live his life in the clouds instead of here o
earth. With her.

She slipped off the engagement ring she'd been wearin
for less than four hours and laid it on the carpet. A plain gol
band with Shay's love attached would have suited her fine.

Then she left him on the floor and huddled in the guest bed she'd used before impulsively jumping back into Shay. She watched the fish swim lazily around the coral until daylight crept through the window.

Shay arranged for the jet to take her back to New Mexico and she left that afternoon without speaking to him again. This was what worry-about-it-tomorrow had gotten her.

Once at home, Juliana took a hot shower and unpacked, then busied herself until she'd cleaned the entire house, restocked the pantry and done all the laundry. Physically and mentally, she was exhausted. Though it was past midnight, she didn't try to go to bed.

The house was hushed. Empty. Lonely. It always had been, even when Eric had lived in it.

She sat at her desk and opened her laptop to work on the parenting book. Why, she had no idea. At some point, she'd have to admit the book wasn't poised to be the blockbuster she'd imagined. Her heart wasn't in it anymore.

Shay's name jumped out from the screen and the eruption in her chest was harsh. She'd broken free of his quicksand, but he'd left grains of that sand all over her. She missed his energy, his whole-face grin. The way he felt under her fingertips.

But he didn't love her. That's what had been different. The whole time.

Letters swirled across the page. Blinking back the moisture, she focused on the screen until the words clarified. "Parenting is foremost a constant compromise, and secondly, a product of sacrifice and commitment."

She'd said almost the same thing to Amanda about true love. Funny how she'd subconsciously connected two very different dynamics.

Or were they different?

She dug out her notes from the hospital and reread the transcript.

"True love is a compromise. You each bring your very best and give one hundred percent to the other. It requires sacrifice and commitment."

Sacrifice and commitment. Words she tossed around when dispassionately discussing how other people should approach parenting and relationships. Yet she'd done neither in her marriage.

She'd done neither with Shay.

Further up the page, Amanda's words jumped out at her, words she hadn't even recalled until now. "I'd like to be with a guy who likes me exactly the way I am. Troy wanted me to be someone I'm not."

Her head swam. She stumbled to the dark kitchen for a drink but the cold water sliding down her dry throat didn't ease the litany in her head.

She was just like Troy.

She'd tried to turn Shay into something he wasn't out of her own need for security and control, and then she'd left him because she couldn't compromise. Not once, but twice.

Anguish slashed at her. She'd hurt him.

You want my heart, too? Too bad. It's still in pieces back in Dallas.

Dr. Cane had brushed that off as latent resentment. Juliana recognized it as the inability to trust her.

Shay had become exactly what she'd thought she wanted—careful. And she hated it.

The empty glass dropped to the counter with a crack. She sank to the floor.

Shay deserved to be with someone who loved him exactly the way he was. Courageous. Bold. Unafraid to grab life with both hands. Unafraid to make hard choices and compromises.

He should be with a woman who didn't try to kill the very thing she loved about him.

Despite the absolute panic and fear at the thought…she wanted to be that woman.

But she wasn't. Not yet. In order to be the right one, she had to change herself.

Until that happened, she couldn't write a book about parenting or be an effective therapist to those who came to her for help. Couldn't heal from the trauma of infertility well enough to be a mother to Mikey. Couldn't be a lover Shay could trust.

She answered questions with questions on purpose, to avoid anything smacking of internal analysis. She despised thinking about her own flaws. Psychologists were supposed to help others, not themselves. The task of altering lifelong habits seemed nearly impossible.

But she'd do it because she had to.

Instinctively, she went to the study and lurched into the chair.

Before long, she had a neatly typed list of steps she would have recommended to a client with this same problem, but then she slammed the laptop lid closed and rested her pounding head on the cool plastic. She couldn't solve this problem with academia. In fact, less thinking would probably help.

Shay. It had always been Shay. He was the only one who could ever pull her out of her own head and all at once, the answer came to her.

She dashed to her room and unearthed the violin. For the first time in eight years, she rosined the bow and drew it across the strings, tuning as she listened to the warm vibrations of the notes.

How blind she'd been. Blind and selfish. Shay had handed her the key and she hadn't even recognized it. As she gave herself over to the music, it flowed through her, releasing the floodgates of her heart. The violin had been her passion but she'd abandoned it—and Shay—in favor of the "plan," the life that made sense but left her hollow and unfulfilled.

The only way to be worthy of Shay was to find the music again.

To find herself.

She played. And played. The notes rolled from her fingers pouring from the strings in a cascade of her secret desires needs, fears. She felt it all, fell headfirst into the blackness rode the wave. Connecting with herself and fulfilling herself instead of searching for someone else to provide her fulfillment.

The music became a time machine, transporting her back to when love had been everything. Then the music became a crystal ball, holding all the answers. She craved connection but feared being left behind and abandoned, so she sought stability at the expense of connection.

Only by letting go could she fully heal. So she let go.

Love without limits coursed through her. Love for Shay.

She loved his confidence, his nerve and selflessness. She loved how he lured her off that ledge and helped her soar She could be Juliana with him, not Dr. Cane, and instead of resisting it because it was scary and illogical and unordered she embraced it.

If she wanted to be happy, if she wanted to be with Shay and make him happy, she had to sacrifice her bent toward self-preservation and become a woman who was enough for a larger-than-life man.

She had to find her courage.

Shay regretted selling the Hayabusa every day, but never so much as today. A long ride through the desert with heavy metal blaring through the headphones in his helmet would be nirvana. Through the window in his home office, he could just barely see the long and winding road stretching out beyond the iron bars surrounding the pool and then disappearing into the mountains.

Emily had the morning off and Mikey was especially

fussy. Plus, Shay was neck-deep in GGS's budget in a last-ditch attempt to shave off some dollars. So he wouldn't have been riding, throttle wide open, anyway.

Blinking, he focused on the unending spreadsheet columns in front of him, but the numbers blurred. Juliana had taken all his energy with her four days ago when he'd drawn the line and she'd stepped all over it without a backward glance.

But GGS's government contract was up soon. He had to come in lower than his competitor's bid or miraculously get a prototype off the ground in record time. Either would save GGS but neither was happening thus far.

And Mikey kept crying no matter what Shay did.

He bounced his leg faster. Slower. Moved the baby to his knees like Juliana had showed him. Nothing worked.

Which was pretty descriptive of everything else, too.

The prototype fuel line was still mysteriously faulty, his competitor was breathing down his neck and the one change he'd wanted to make—marrying Juliana—had been thrown back in his face. His entire life he'd faced down challenges, refusing to balk. He'd have to do the same this time, if he could figure out how.

Fifteen minutes later, Shay set Mikey down inside the ExerSaucer next to his chair, still screaming, and handed him a chunky cardboard book. The baby immediately stuck it in his mouth, drooled a bunch and quieted down.

Shay rolled his eyes. A book. That was the secret to silence?

He swiveled his chair front and center to sort through the budget numbers—again—but something hit his leg and he glanced down. The baby banged the book on Shay's leg a few more times and looked up through Grant's eyes.

He wondered how it was possible for his heart to ache so badly when it surely had taken all the torture it could handle.

"What?" he said to the baby, who zeroed in on Shay's face with rapt baby fascination. "You think I handled everything with her wrong? Tell me what I should have done. I'm going to get in that prototype at some point. I'm going to climb rocks and drive fast. I can't be someone else."

Juliana couldn't even *see* that she didn't love the real Shay.

Mikey blew spit bubbles and coaxed a smile out of Shay. With a "gah," Mikey handed him the book.

"A peace offering?" Gingerly, Shay took the wet book by the corners. *Goodnight Moon*. Juliana's favorite.

His eyes began to burn. He could still feel her in his arms, smell her in his sleep. Good thing he'd never given her another chance to rip his heart out. Otherwise, being alone, being without her, would *really* suck.

She'd sat in his lap in this very chair, poking him into admitting—into remembering—he had courage to spare. He didn't feel so courageous right now.

His phone beeped and he glanced at it. Email from Cal Blankenship. After handing Mikey the book, Shay scrolled through the message. To the best of the executive staff's legal ability, they'd put together a number they were confident would win GGS the contract renewal. Shay did the math instantly for what they'd have to cut from the budget.

A pounding headache started up at the base of his skull. It was a lot of zeros. A *lot*.

Mikey banged his leg again with the book. *Goodnight Moon*.

Yeah. That was the answer. He had to put his courage to the ultimate test.

He had to say good-night to the moon, stars, space, orbital flight—all of it. As excruciating as it was, Juliana had been correct about one thing. His life had become something new without his permission, without giving him a moment to acclimate, but it was time he became a new man along with it. A man who could make sacrifices which were actually sacrifices. Painful, difficult and necessary. But for the best.

Within thirty minutes, the budget-cut number from Cal's

email matched the number on Shay's spreadsheet, down to the last zero. Before he could change his mind, Shay replied to the email detailing a strategy to redo materials procurement from one-year to five-year contracts fronted with his own personal money. Risky, because he'd be locked in to purchasing expensive raw material he wouldn't need if his competitor won. But the cost savings would be worth it if it worked.

The next paragraph outlined his plan to sell the GGS building in Fort Worth and move the company to West Texas where a space port facility sat empty and could be used to house operations.

As a bonus, he would no longer have to fly anything to work. Not that Juliana would be around to appreciate how he'd used the extra dose of daring that she'd seen in him—

He went cold and then hot as the truth hit him.

Juliana had prodded him into admitting he had courage—because she *knew* him and saw right into his heart.

She'd encouraged him to use what was at his core in a constructive way, by channeling it into his company instead of into dangerous pastimes. Not because she wanted him to be someone else, but someone better. A father, husband and the sole founding member of GGS still living.

He'd thanked her by stubbornly keeping her at arm's length.

"I did handle everything with Juliana wrong."

Mikey waved a fist in a circle and drooled. Shay took it as the equivalent of baby applause and smiled. It wasn't Grant's approval, but it was close enough.

His phone beeped, turning his stomach over. That was fast. The board must have loved his proposal to respond so quickly. He glanced at the screen and then did a double take. Not Cal.

Juliana.

He opened the message. It was an attached video. Intrigued, he opened the file, half hoping it was that striptease he'd never received.

Weepy, passionate music poured from the phone's speaker as Juliana played the violin he'd given her. Pure emotion radiated from her as she drew the bow over the strings. She *was* the music.

Turned out his heart wasn't in pieces on the floor of her dorm room. It thumped in his chest, keeping pace with the notes. Despite everything he'd told himself, promised himself, lied to himself about, he'd never gotten over Juliana Cane. Couldn't have, because he was still in love with that girl he'd first seen play the violin all those years ago.

She'd called him. She'd come back from New Mexico because she wanted to be with him. Told him she loved him with zero reassurance he felt the same way. She'd started playing the violin again and sent him this video.

Juliana constantly showed courage in the face of his closed heart.

What had he done? Resisted entertaining the idea of trusting her again. So convinced she'd disappoint him, he'd refused to give her makeover enough credit, offered shallow compromises and refused to give her a real second chance. Refused to consider forgiving her.

What if he had?

With Mikey in his lap, both of them mesmerized, they watched the video three times on his computer.

The video could mean a million things. It could be an invitation to another broken heart. But he wouldn't let that fear win.

Yes, Juliana had walked away—again—but this time he was going to follow her.

Thirteen

Juliana hadn't seen Shay in five days, not since realizing if she was going to lose him anyway, she'd rather do it on her terms.

When he rang the bell, she flung open the door and drank in the sight of the man who'd taken her to heights she'd never dreamed possible. No standard, polite greeting could possibly convey all the things in her heart, so she settled for, "I've been expecting you."

"Yeah?" He cleared his throat. "It was just a video. How did you know I'd come?"

She smiled and opened the door wider, motioning him inside. "You're the only person in the world who cares enough to unscramble my code."

The video had been a message—*I'll make the first move if you'll make the second*. A gamble, but obviously a good one.

Shay was here.

She wanted to dissolve in his arms, feel his solid warmth and strength. She'd missed it so much. But they needed to talk first. A lot and with painful honesty. When she was through, there was a very good possibility he wouldn't give her another chance.

But for now, he was here and she'd do everything in her power to convince him she was worth the risk.

"So that's what it was?" Shay asked. "A code?"

He followed her into the living room and settled into the plush navy couch, her violin lying on the coffee table in front of him. Juliana chose to join him without hesitation. The couch was built for two people but the few inches between them felt like an impassible ocean of cushion.

"I answered the question myself," she said. "About why you bought me the violin. It took me a while. Thank you. What you gave me…I can never repay you."

Heart and mind open, she met his gaze and prayed he could see straight through her, straight into her anguish over hurting him, into her gratefulness for the gift. Into the fathomless love she'd rediscovered.

Arms crossed over his T-shirt, he shrugged. "It was just a violin."

His expression gave away nothing of his thoughts. Walking away from him had been necessary, but hadn't come without a price. His heart and mind were shuttered tight.

"No. It's not. Like the video wasn't just a video. You and I are so similar, it's hard to reconcile how we can talk but not communicate."

"Similar? We're the least similar people on the planet. That's what got us to this point."

At least he was talking, which was more than she deserved. Her fingers ached to reach for him but she laced them in her lap. "I never could figure out why you played classical music all the time. Guitars and mean thumping bass seems more your style. Then when I picked up that bow and started to play, I realized. The music was your own version of code. Am I wrong?"

He grew so still, she forgot to breathe. Then something shifted in his posture, in the air. In his soul, if she could be so lucky. He searched her face, his eyes liquid and earnest.

"Ju, I gave you the violin because the first time I heard you play, that was it. You hit me right here." He took her hand and placed it flat against his heart. Her fingers pressed against the faint *lub-lub*. "And never let go. That girl played with such unrestrained passion. Somewhere over time, you lost that. I wanted you to have it back."

Tears gathered in her eyes and instead of blinking them back, she let them spill. "I insisted to myself that I didn't like how you pulled me out of my ordered, academic world. That I was too frightened of all the dark emotions you make me feel. But I was drawn to it more and more because you were allowing me to put Dr. Cane away and be Juliana again. I pretended you had to drag me into your chaos, swearing I didn't want it. I lied. When I reclaimed the music, I reclaimed the ability to admit I want it all. With you."

He watched her with an intense focus, and with the pad of his thumb, brushed the tears away. "I like the sound of that."

"My capacity for self-preservation is well documented. It's what drove me away from you. Both times. I couldn't risk instability and tried to remake you into that stable force. I'm sorry."

She shut her eyes for a beat and started to drop her hand, but he pressed it harder against his chest, refusing to let her go. Refusing to let her look away.

"But Ju, don't you see? You're *my* stability. You were always there, on the ground, steadying me. Giving me a place to land. You're the earth to my sky."

"Oh, you decided to give me poetry after all?" And then her throat closed and she couldn't speak.

She provided stability for *him*. It was inconceivable, like she'd finally reached the Emerald City only to hear Glinda the good witch tell her the way home had been on her feet the entire time.

His mouth lifted up into a small smile. "You're the only one who ever could inspire poetry."

As lovely as poetry was, they weren't finished with the hard part of the conversation. "Shay, why did you ask me to marry you? Truthfully."

"Truth?" Discomfort flashed across his face, tightening his mouth. "I told myself the idea of marrying you scared me. Fear is my worst enemy. To avoid being controlled by it, I stare down whatever scary thing is before me and never blink. So I looked you in the eye and proposed. It was a handy way to keep you around without any risk on my part."

"You're never afraid. You're the bravest person I know."

He shook his head and dark caramel-shot locks of hair fell into his face. No ball cap today. "Courage is moving forward even when you're scared. So here's another bit of truth for you. I wasn't afraid of marrying you. I was afraid of loving you. I came today because I couldn't let that fear of loving you hold me back."

Relief filled some of the empty space inside. "So where are we?"

"Where do you want to be?"

She had to laugh. "Answering questions with questions. And you say we're not similar."

She'd forced him to dance around the land mines. She'd gladly run through the field and detonate all of them at once. She owed him and he deserved it.

She cupped his jaw. Stubble scraped at her palm and it lifted a weight she'd carried inside forever. "I'm sorry I tried to change you. I don't want you to be anyone else but Shay. I'm finally brave enough to let you be yourself and brave enough to face it if something happens to you. Replace your cars and motorcycles. Plan a rock climbing trip. Do what makes *you* happy. My insecurities are what drove you to be-

ieve you'd lose the suit. You won't, regardless of whether
ou slow down. If you can forgive me, I'd like to see if we
an try again. For real."

He was a package deal, she reminded herself. "Before you
ay anything, keep in mind you have Mikey to consider. In
ll things." Shay's hand was still in hers and she squeezed it.
Infertility was a slow leech on my soul but I'm finally in a
lace where I can heal. I can't promise I'll be a good mom
o your son. I want to try. But you should consider my limi-
ations before you think about giving me a second chance."

He snorted. "What limitations? Ju, any kid would be lucky
o have you as a mom."

"I'm a mess." Her lips were trembling. "I don't know how
o be a good mother."

In response, Shay drew her off the couch, then positioned
er in front of the mirror hanging in the foyer. "Look."

He stood directly behind her, hair untamed and five days
f stubble darkening his jaw. So gorgeously rough and wild.
lis vibrating masculinity—the full force if it—warmed her
ack. It took an extreme amount of will not to melt into it.

"Don't look at me," Shay corrected with a smile. "Look
t you. Cool. Unruffled. Nothing fazes you. That's the mom
want for my son."

Mom. She took in her smooth hair, crisp tailored skirt and
hirt and saw Dr. Cane, the proficient therapist who tried to
eplace the baby she'd never conceived with other people's
hildren.

"Stay there." Shay disappeared and returned to place the
iolin in her hands. "Now look again. There's a woman who
nderstands passion and all the depths of emotion possible.
:specially courage. That's also the mom I want for my son.
)ld Juliana and New Juliana in one package."

More tears spilled down her cheeks and she watched the
voman in the mirror cry. She barely recognized herself. In-
ide or out. She'd accepted a job to teach him how to be a fa-

ther, but those components were already an integral part o
Shay. Instead, she was learning from him how to be a mother

She set the violin on the table in the foyer and met his gaz
squarely. "I can never give you children with your DNA. Wil
you be okay with that?"

His brows lifted. "I want you to be the mother of *all* m
children. However they come to us. I did some poking aroun
into experimental procedures being done in Switzerland, spe
cifically for women who haven't responded to IVF. There'
surrogacy, too. The entire world of medical science is ope
to you. Or we can adopt. If you want to."

The entire world. Her heart nearly burst with the possi
bilities.

"Are you scared?" Shay asked in her ear and she nodded
"Me, too. That means we have to move forward."

His arms came up, encircling her. Holding her. Catch
ing her as she fell into those crystal-clear green eyes watch
ing her in the mirror. He'd never let her face her nightmare
alone. That made all the difference. Infertility hadn't been a
curse, but a challenge she could overcome and put behind her

There was no way she could resist any longer. She sagge
back against his hard frame, and his lips grazed her temple

"Moving forward sounds good," she said.

"Here's the thing." His warm breath fanned her hairline
"The changes you asked me to make were sacrifices. Bu
necessary ones because Mikey needs me to be around fo
him. I'm sitting there pissed off because I couldn't jump o
a bike or go fly a plane but, Ju, when you left, I realized tha
when you were with me, I never had the urge to do any o
those things."

She started to respond but he closed her mouth with a gen
tle finger to her lips.

"It's still my turn," he said. "I asked you to teach me how
to be a father. Wanna know what I learned?"

She nodded.

"I can only be the dad Mikey needs, only be worthy of rant's faith in me, as long as you're providing my foundaon. Everyone wants to feel secure and you do that for me. ou keep me stable. I can't be the man you see unless you're ere. I can't be a good father without you."

"I don't know what to say."

"Sure you do. What's in your heart? Say it, Ju. Out loud. hat makes it real."

The words tumbled from her lips without restraint. "I love ou. Exactly the way you are. If you'll forgive me and find way to trust me again, I'll gladly kiss you goodbye every norning as you fly off in your helicopter and never say another word about it. Can you give me another chance?"

"No helicopters or spaceships. I'm addicted to that adrenane rush and you're it, all day long, every day. You've always een more than enough for me. Hopefully I can convince you f it by telling you I sold the building in Fort Worth and we're noving all of GGS's operations to the space port facility."

Her pulse faltered. "Why would you do that? Shay, space your dream. You can't give it up."

"My dream is to be up in the stars and I'm there every time look in your eyes. You taught me that love is about making al sacrifices. So I did. I want you to be happy, because, Ju, love you, too," he murmured in her ear and in the mirror, is face and his beautiful green irises radiated with it. "Alays have. Always will."

"No, Shay. Keep operations in the space port facility for ow, but work on the spaceship and get it into orbit. I refuse compromise on this."

"You refuse, huh?" He smiled that whole-face smile she ved. "What if I let someone else test it and wait until it's approved for commercial use before I take my first ride? That's e only compromise I'll agree to."

"That's quite a compromise," she croaked. "I don't have nything nearly as good to offer in return."

"That's not true. Play your violin for me once in a while
He pursed his lips. "Better yet, I believe there was some dis
cussion about a striptease. Figure out a way to combine th
two, and we'll call it even."

She laughed through the tears, which wouldn't stop. "I'
consider it."

He growled and spun her in his arms. "Consider this."

And then he crushed his mouth to hers and flung her o
the cliff with his unique brand of chaotic, exhilarating, whol
body love, exactly the way she wanted.

Epilogue

Juliana packed her suitcases—again—and flew back to West Texas. She and Shay had a blissful week together before Juliana's leave of absence expired. Per Shay's suggestion, she then saw clients in New Mexico the first half of the week and hopped the jet back home for the remainder of the week. Shay had begun the long, complicated task of moving his headquarters and they often missed each other. The anticipation of seeing each other again after several days of separation made for some pretty good times.

For once, they were both home for the weekend and had invited the Greenes for a visit. After a morning of baby-centric activities, the four adults and Mikey relaxed on the back patio after lunch.

Juliana scooped up Mikey from his bouncy seat and passed him to Mrs. Greene. The baby examined the reading glasses around his grandmother's neck with sticky fingers. The older woman laughed.

"He's so inquisitive. His father was the same way." Mrs.

Greene grimaced. "I mean Grant. It will be hard to remem
ber he has a new father now."

A week ago, Shay, Juliana and the Greenes had sat dow
for a frank conversation without lawyers. Juliana spoke fro
her heart about wishing to provide Mikey with a mother an
father who loved him. The Greenes admitted grief had le
to decisions that weren't serving the baby's best interest
and agreed to drop the petition in exchange for a standin
invitation to visit Mikey. Slowly, everyone acclimated to th
arrangement, and the baby allowed his grandmother to hol
him for longer and longer periods of time.

Shay smiled and snaked a casual hand around Juliana
waist, setting the glider they shared in motion. "Mikey shou
think of Grant as his father. He's got more than one set o
grandparents, right? There's no law that says he can't hav
two fathers."

The casual hand wandered into the waistband of Juliana
skirt, and she shot him a sidelong glance. They'd disappeare
on the Greenes once today already, during Mikey's nap, b
the older couple had very kindly failed to mention it.

Mr. Greene cleared his throat. "We appreciate your wil
ingness to be open with Mikey about his biological parent
This situation has been difficult on everyone and we're read
to let bygones be bygones."

It was as close to an apology as Shay would likely get b
the light in his vibrant green eyes told her he'd take it. He no
ded to Mr. Greene. "We appreciate you spending time wit
Mikey this afternoon. Juliana has an important errand to run

Her stomach flipped. Yes, it was time.

From the back of her closet in the master bath, Julian
pulled out jeans and a T-shirt and then dug through her boxe
from college, which she'd stored in an extra bedroom. In th
third box, she found the picture she sought: a younger, care
free Juliana squeezed into a booth at a Mexican restauran

ay's arm slung around her shoulders. Grant and Donna
re on Shay's left, mugging for the camera.

Grant and Donna had left her behind once again, to a place
e couldn't follow. But Shay was still here, ready to catch
r at a moment's notice.

Until Mrs. Greene had mentioned a picture, Juliana had
rgotten she'd had one. She touched Donna's face with her
ngertip. "Don't worry. I'll be a good mom to your son. I
omise to love him as much as you did."

She tucked the picture into her pocket and hustled Shay
to the Land Rover. He drove to the outskirts of Abilene, to
e place she'd located online—Adventure Park. She bought
e ticket. The black letters on the pass burned her retinas
she stared at it.

Zero Gravity Bungee Jump.

She watched a few others jump before she could force her
uscles to climb the seven stories to the platform. All the
hers lived. She would, too.

Her mind drained as she stepped out on the platform. The
lon safety straps cut off all her air and she couldn't breathe.
e touched the picture in her pocket and it steadied her.

Do it. She edged further out until she could see the stunt-
an airbag on the ground below, which the operator had as-
red her was rated for falls from much higher up than seven
ories.

Then she took flight, falling, hair whipping, wind whis-
ng. Her heart stopped. It didn't beat again until the cord
apped her backward and then it was real.

Shay waited for her at the airbag's exit. She fell into his
ms and he held her close. "I would have jumped with you."

"I know." Her chest heaved against his, heart pounding
d adrenaline flying through her veins. "I had to do it for
yself."

She'd hated it and it wasn't fun, but love wasn't about se-
rity—it was a free fall from ten thousand feet and now

she was ready to embrace it. Ready to write a book abo
the crazy, messy thing called parenting and how the on
way to get through it was to love children without restrai
no matter what.

"I'm proud of you," he said gruffly. "Do you have to
jump out of a plane next, or can I put this on you?"

He held up the plain gold band he'd kept all these yea
and she nodded.

"Yes. Now I'll marry you. And sign the adoption paper:
They'd be adopting Mikey together, and be a real family.

Shay and Juliana flew to Cabo San Lucas a week la
and married on the beach. Mikey, with Emily's help, w
the ring bearer and when Shay slipped the band on Julian
finger, she curled her hand into a fist. The metal was wa
with Shay's love.

Sometimes you gave up things you'd dreamed about
years—and for your sacrifice, you got something far, far b
ter in return.

* * * * *

s far as Stern was concerned, his best friend had lost her
er-loving mind. But he didn't say that. Instead, he asked,
What's his name?"

"You don't need to know that. Do you tell me the name
every woman you want?"

"This is different."

"Really? In what way?"

He wasn't sure, but he just knew that it was. "For you
even ask me, that means you're not ready for the kind of
lationship you're going after."

JoJo threw her head back and laughed. "Stern, I'll be
irty next year. I'm beginning to think that most of the men
town wonder if I'm really a girl."

He studied her. There had never been any doubt in his
ind that she was a girl. She had long lashes and eyes so
rk they were the color of midnight. She had gorgeous
gs, long and endless. But he knew he was one of the few
en who'd ever seen them.

"You hide what a nice body you have," he finally said.
e suddenly sat up straight in the rocker. "I have an idea.

What you need is a makeover."

"A makeover?"

"Yes, and then you need to go where your guy hangs out. In a dress that shows your legs, in a style that shows off your hair." He reached over and took the cap off her head. Lustrous dark brown hair tumbled to her shoulders. He smiled. "See, I like it already."

And he did. He was tempted to run his hands through to feel the silky texture.

He leaned back and took another sip of his beer, wondering where such a tempting thought had come from. This was JoJo, for heaven's sake. His best friend. He should not be thinking about how silky her hair was.

He should not be bothered by the thought of men checking out JoJo, of men calling her for a date.

Suddenly, he was thinking that maybe a makeover wasn't such a great idea after all.

Will Stern help JoJo win her dream man?

STERN

by New York Times *and* USA TODAY
bestselling author Brenda Jackson

Available September 2013
Only from Harlequin® Desire!

Desire

ALWAYS POWERFUL, PASSIONATE AND PROVOCATIVE.

THE NANNY TRAP
Cat Schield

*A Billionaires & Babies novel: Powerful men...
wrapped around their babies' little fingers*

When his wife deserts their child, Blake hires the baby's
surrogate mother as nanny—and desire unexpectedly
ignites between them. But when the nanny reveals her
secret, everything changes!

Look for *THE NANNY TRAP* next month by
Cat Schield, only from Harlequin® Desire.

Available wherever books and ebooks are sold.

HARLEQUIN®

Desire

ALWAYS POWERFUL, PASSIONATE AND PROVOCATIVE.

CONVENIENTLY
HIS PRINCESS

Olivia Gates

**Part of the Married by Royal Decree series:
When the king commands, they say "I do!"**

Aram's convenient bride turns out to be most
inconvenient when he falls in love with her! But will
Kanza believe in their love when the truth comes out?

Find out next month in
CONVENIENTLY HIS PRINCESS by Olivia Gates,
only from Harlequin® Desire.

Available wherever books and ebooks are sold.

Love the Harlequin book you just read?

Your opinion matters.

Review this book on your favorite
book site, review site, blog or your own
social media properties and share
your opinion with other readers!

Be sure to connect with us at:
Harlequin.com/Newsletters
Facebook.com/HarlequinBooks
Twitter.com/HarlequinBooks

HARLEQUIN®

A *Romance* FOR EVERY MOOD

**Stay up-to-date on all your
romance-reading news with the
Harlequin Shopping Guide,
featuring bestselling authors, exciting new
miniseries, books to watch and more!**

The newest issue will be delivered right to you
with our compliments! There are 4 each year.

Signing up is easy.

EMAIL

ShoppingGuide@Harlequin.ca

WRITE TO US

HARLEQUIN BOOKS
Attention: Customer Service Department
P.O. Box 9057, Buffalo, NY 14269-9057

OR PHONE

1-800-873-8635 in the United States
1-888-343-9777 in Canada

Please allow 4-6 weeks for delivery of the first issue by mail.